MURDER CON CARNE

A Mexican Café Cozy Mystery

Holly Plum

Copyright © 2016 by Holly Plum

All rights reserved. No part of this publication may be reproduced, stored in or introduced into a retrieval system, or transmitted, in any form, or by any means (electronic, mechanical, photocopying, recording, or otherwise) without the prior written permission of the copyright owner of this book.

This is a work of fiction. Names, characters, places, brands, media, and incidents are either the product of the author's imagination or are used fictitiously. Any resemblance to actual persons, living or dead, business establishments, events, or locales is entirely coincidental.

The author acknowledges the trademarked status and trademark owners of various products referenced in this work of fiction, which have been used without permission. The publication/use of these trademarks is not authorized, associated with, or sponsored by the trademark owners.

CHAPTER ONE

Mari Ramirez swore quietly as she pulled into the parking lot of her family's Mexican restaurant. Her brothers, Alex and David, were supposed to have opened it by now. But of course, the restaurant was empty. Steve Wilson, the meat delivery man, stood near the glass doors with his hands in the pockets of his oversized jeans. He casually smoked his cigarette. Mari wondered why he hadn't moved to the back of his truck where it was cooler. Summer mornings in Texas could be vicious. Sweat was already dripping down Steve's neck.

Steve held up one hand as Mari emerged from her car. It was a half-wave, half-salute. Mari's bulldog leaped out of the passenger's seat and began growling. Tabasco was not a fan of most delivery men, especially Steve.

"Tabasco, hush," Mari said sternly. Mari's dad hated it when she brought him inside, but Mari knew better than to leave a dog in a parked car on a warm summer day. Tabasco peered out from behind Mari's ankles and glared with all the might he could muster. He hated Steve and Tabasco took the opportunity to make his feelings known whenever he saw him.

"Took one of ya long enough," Steve commented, though he didn't sound angry. "I'm almost positive your dad's in there, but either he can't hear me or he's too busy to come to the door."

"That sounds like Dad." Mari jangled her keys by way of apology. "He usually shuts the door and tunes out the world when he goes over the accounts."

"Sometimes I think he *sleeps* here," Steve responded.

"Well, that's the way we do things at Lito Bueno's Mexican Restaurant."

Steve laughed as Mari unlocked the door. In the reflection of the glass, she saw the sun glinting brightly with the arid, blue sky around it. A single red pickup truck sat parked across the street at the Lucky Noodle, her least favorite restaurant, and her family's main competitor. For twenty years Mr. Chun, owner of the Lucky Noodle, had been trying to run them out of business with no luck. The town had one Mexican restaurant and one Chinese restaurant, and that was how people liked it.

The lock had jammed, and it was only after several minutes of patient coaxing and a few minutes of impatient knocking, that Mari was able to pry it open. It was a relief to be in that cool room. Not just because of the heat but because the tension between her and Steve was like a third wheel that followed them wherever they went. Steve had liked Mari since her first year of college, and he had asked her out once. She'd said no, and

Steve had never quite gotten over it. Now and then, when he thought no one was paying attention, a flicker of that old yearning would glimmer in his eyes for a moment. Mari was instinctively kind to him, half out of genuine affection and half out of pity.

As Steve made his way to the freezer, Mari took in the whole room with a single glance. When she was a little girl, her brothers had often gotten her into trouble by daring her to run around the restaurant in the middle of business hours. They would set up their own obstacle courses and take turns trying to dash from one end of the room to the other, amid the square tables with their red tops and the long-legged strangers who were constantly getting up and sitting down again. Whoever made it all the way back without bumping into someone or being caught by their dad would get a prize. The prizes varied—anything from bubblegum to cherry soda. It was well worth the spanking she had gotten when they'd gotten home that night.

In an hour or two people would begin pouring into the restaurant for lunch. The tables would be stacked with steaming plates of paella, homemade tortillas, enchiladas, chile rellenos, and the overhead speakers would play traditional Mexican music. At that moment, however, Mari heard nothing but the clicking of a calculator coming from a back office.

Mari walked into the office, Tabasco tagging along at her heels.

"Didn't you hear me knocking?" Mari said by way of introduction.

"I thought you were Steve," her father replied, without bothering to glance up from his books. "What is that dog doing in my office?"

"He followed me inside. I told him no, but he just wouldn't listen."

José Ramirez let out a deep sigh. "You know the problem with kids these days? They don't respect their elders."

This was an argument they had been having for so long that by now it was almost a game. Mari played the role of the difficult child while her father feigned world-weariness.

"I bet things were better back in Mexico, huh?" Mari commented.

"They were," José stated. "When you told a woman to do something, she did it."

"Okay, Dad." Patting him lightly on the shoulder, Mari turned and left the office. Her father was an old-fashioned man with dated ideas about a woman's role.

Steve emerged from the freezer as Mari filled up the napkin dispensers. He was out of breath, and his black-and-yellow protective gloves were covered with small shards of ice. As she had done so many times before, Mari took pity on him.

"Hey, before you go," she said, "I think we have some Carne Asada left over from last night."

Steve grinned shyly. "You know I don't speak Mexican, Mari. What does that mean?"

"It's meat that's been marinated," Mari answered. "I'll warm some up for you with a side of rice and beans."

Mari walked past her dad's office, and he flung open his door.

"Don't encourage that boy," José growled as he glanced at the kitchen. Mr. Ramirez wasn't a fan of freebies, and he could spot them a mile away.

"Relax, Dad," Mari assured him. "It's just a small plate of food."

"Marisol, how many times do I have to say it?" José was one of the few people who still called Mari by her full name. "Every penny counts."

Mari nodded, acknowledging that she understood. She then quickly made Steve a plate of food anyway.

Steve sat at the back of the restaurant, eating the meal with a hungry relish. Maybe it was because he hadn't eaten all morning or maybe it was Mari's unexpected display of kindness, but for some reason, Steve seemed happier than usual. Most mornings he skulked to the freezer like a man with no purpose. This morning he seemed cheery, and more alert.

Mari left Steve to his food and finished filling up the napkin dispensers. With a jingle of bells, the front door opened and Mateo the bus boy came into the room. Shrugging sleepily, Mateo slung his backpack down behind the counter.

"Hola," Mari said brightly, determined not to be intimidated by his gruff manner.

"Hola, yourself," Mateo replied as he washed his hands. Mateo was in his mid-thirties, but his baby face made him look more like a high-schooler.

It was clear that Mateo had been up late the night before. Judging from the circles under his eyelids, Mari was inclined to suspect he hadn't slept at all. She tried to think of a delicate way to approach the subject as they filled the salt and pepper shakers.

"So, are you dating anyone?" she asked him. Mateo's last relationship had flamed out in spectacular fashion when his girlfriend admitted to working for the Lucky Noodle. Mr. Chun, the owner, had paid her a considerable sum of money to learn the secret family salsa recipe. He had planned to offer it in his buffet just to spite Mari's father.

"I'm not with that same nutbag anymore if that's what you're asking," Mateo responded, though he seemed to be studiously avoiding her gaze as he said this.

"I was just making conversation," Mari said, over the yapping of Tabasco from the other side of the restaurant. Mateo managed a small smile.

At that moment, Mr. Ramirez rushed out of the office looking as grumpy as ever. "Mari, would you silence that animal? Do whatever you have to do. I *don't* care." With an ominous gleam of malice, he crept back inside.

Mari ran out of the kitchen, past the bar and into the cool dining room. She prepared herself mentally to have to pull Tabasco away from some enraged customer. But there were no customers in the restaurant at this hour. That is to say; there were no live ones. The half-finished remains of last night's Carne Asada were sitting on a table at the back of the room.

And under the table lay the body of Steve Wilson.

CHAPTER TWO

Two hours had passed, and Lito Bueno's Mexican Restaurant was already closed for the day. But the dining room was not empty. A small team of detectives was gathered around the body, taking pictures and collecting evidence. An unfriendly looking woman in a gray coat who couldn't have been much older than Mari walked slowly through the restaurant with a phone in one hand. She appeared to be recording the crime scene.

"Is she even allowed to be here?" asked Mr. Ramirez. He was upset because the restaurant had been forced to close for the day.

"She is, Dad," Mari answered. "She's collecting evidence."

Her father sniffed disapprovingly as if to insinuate that where he came from, women knew better than to become police detectives. Between this and the fact that he seemed more concerned about the business than a man's death, Mari was beginning to feel annoyed.

"I don't know what *you're* so upset about, anyway," she said in her most sarcastic voice. "The whole family gets a day off, and business is going to go through the roof. Everyone will want to eat at Lito Bueno's. I bet they'll be lining up to sit in the chair Steve was stabbed in."

"Forgive me if I don't share your enthusiasm," Mr. Ramirez replied. "And you shouldn't speak of the dead like that."

"I have to joke about it." But Mari stopped short of explaining why. Thinking about her friend being murdered while she stood in the other room filling salt shakers with Mateo was too much to process. Mari would reflect on it when she was alone and not surrounded by reporters and policemen. "Anyway, you don't look too sad yourself."

But Mr. Ramirez barely seemed to be listening. "What happened was very tragic." He said it in an unconvincing tone. "If your brothers had been at work when they were supposed to be, it might never have happened."

"Yeah, where were they?" Mari asked.

José shrugged. "Hopefully this will teach them. How many times have I said we must never leave the dining hall unattended during business hours?"

"I don't think anyone was expecting a murder," Mari commented.

"Well, that's what happened. And now the rest of us are going to have to deal with it."

Mari felt unprepared to handle the subject of death. One minute Steve was alive and then he was gone. Mari wondered if the dead body at the back of the restaurant could have been hers. Even her father, for all his mercenary considerations, stared soberly through the window of his office into the dining room as though contemplating his own mortality.

Mari felt the regret that came from knowing she could have treated the dead with more kindness. Dating Steve Wilson was never an option, but she remembered all the times she and Alex had laughed about him and called him names behind his back. Even the fact that she had fed him a meal that morning didn't make up for it.

As if the situation wasn't already frightening enough, there was the possibility that Steve had been murdered by someone she knew. The police were treating the case as a criminal investigation. They would probably press charges. But against whom? Who did Mari know that could be a killer? Mateo had been with her the whole time. Her dad had been in his office, and in any case, he wasn't a killer.

Who did that leave?

An officer whose dark uniform seemed too tight for his large belly came toward them. His hair was graying at the edges, and his eyes were small and beady. The loose network of red veins running around their edges looked like the map of a city. He coughed as he approached.

"I'm Detective Price," the man said, extending one hand to Mari and then to her father, who shook it in turn. "I'll need to interview both of you separately. You can decide which of you wants to go first. Also, can I borrow your office, Mr. Ramirez?"

Mr. Ramirez seemed less than enthusiastic about having to relinquish his private space, but Detective Price didn't wait for his permission. Mari chose to go first. The detective followed her into the office and closed the door.

"How long had you known the victim?" he asked when they were both settled.

"Since college," Mari said. "He was a few years older than me, but we met while I was working here during the summers to put myself through school. He asked me out once. I don't think he had ever had a girlfriend."

"And you made it clear you weren't interested?"

"Yes, not that it stopped him from trying," Mari answered.

"Can you elaborate?" The detective waited.

"Oh, nothing huge. He would just find ways to do nice things for me. Flowers left in my dad's office. Chocolates. Framed photographs. You know..."

"But you wouldn't describe his behavior as threatening or stalker-like," the detective added

"No, he was harmless," Mari answered honestly.

"What did the rest of your family think of him?"

"They often made jokes about him," Mari confessed, feeling the guilt churning in her stomach.

"What kind of jokes?"

"Not so nice things. Please, don't make me say them. I feel bad enough about it now that he's dead." Mari felt the heat rising into her face.

"Fair enough," Detective Price agreed. "Tell me about your dad, Ms. Ramirez."

"What about him?" Mari tilted her head curiously,

"What did he think of the victim?" The detective waited in earnest, studying Mari's every movement.

"Honestly, he didn't think much of Steve. I mean, he's messed up our meat orders more than once. Hopefully, it isn't a rude thing to say about him but Steve wasn't that great at his job."

Mari was getting flustered and feared she wasn't fully in control of her senses. She also couldn't help noticing how determined Detective Price was to bring the subject back around to her dad.

"But your father," he said. "Did he ever express frustration towards the victim? Anger? Did he ever lash out at him?"

Mari shook her head, struggling to keep her composure. "He would mumble things under his breath. That was as mean as he ever got."

"What kinds of things?" the detective asked.

"One time he called him a *big banana head* when Steve locked the keys to the freezer inside the freezer. Honestly, he could've said a lot worse."

"Was Steve what you would call a jokester?"

"Not particularly," Mari answered. "The whole key thing was an accident."

"Was he clumsy? Accident-prone?" The detective jotted a few things down.

"In the extreme," Mari said. "We used to joke that he wouldn't know which shoes to put on which feet if someone didn't write it down."

"*Did* someone write it down?"

"No, it was just a joke." Mari wrinkled her nose, annoyed by the detective's questions.

"Did Steve ever show signs of depression?" Detective Price continued.

Mari had to think about that one. "Not around me. I guess if I were him, I would've been depressed, just because of the nature of my life, you know? But if he was, he never showed it."

"What did the other staff members think of him?"

Mari shook her head slowly. "You would have to ask them."

Detective Price had kept his attention studiously fixed on his notepad throughout the interview. As Mari watched him writing, a new thought occurred to her. "We are talking about a murder here, aren't we? Not a suicide?"

"Ms. Ramirez," the detective replied, setting down his pen and paper and looking at her directly for the first time. "At this moment, I honestly don't know, and I think it would be useless to speculate. A few hours ago a man was found dead in the back of your restaurant, a knife sticking out of his back. Obviously, given the manner of his death, suicide seems unlikely. But that leaves us with the other possibility, the one that no one here wants to face, or admit to."

"What's that?" Mari asked.

"That a murder has taken place at your family's restaurant," Detective Price answered, "and my leading suspect is your father."

CHAPTER THREE

David and Alex finally showed up for work two hours later. Neither of them had a convincing explanation for where they had been. They were both surprised to learn that a murder had taken place at the restaurant in their absence.

"This is your fault," José Ramirez shouted, as the two brothers stared at the bloody floor. "If you'd been here when you were supposed to be, no one would've died, and we wouldn't be losing an entire day's worth of business."

"Sorry," David answered. "Me and Alex were…"

Silence fell over the restaurant as everyone waited for David to conclude the sentence. After this had gone on for two or three minutes, Mr. Ramirez shoved his hands into his pockets. And with a disgruntled snort, he returned to his back office.

By now, news of the murder had spread throughout the small town. Steve Wilson had no family to speak of, and no friends. Yet, everyone in town had a story about the time they had run into him stocking the freezer section of the local grocery store or beaten him at poker, or found him ripping apart a whole loaf of bread to feed to the geese that ran through Birchwood Park. A spontaneous crowd had gathered in the street between Lito Bueno's Mexican restaurant and the Lucky Noodle, singing songs and looking solemn. An old woman to whom Steve had been especially kind had arranged rose petals in the shape of a beef steak. Inside the petals the townsfolk placed candles and pennies, and anything else they thought might convey their respects. Steve Wilson had turned out to be more popular in death than he had ever been in life.

"I don't get it," David said, watching the scene through the window. "A man dies, and suddenly everyone pretends they were his best friend. I just don't get it."

"He was murdered," Alex added. "No one likes to admit it, but everyone loves a good murder."

"Is there such a thing?" David wrinkled his nose.

No one replied. Mari was getting restless having to wait here while the police conducted their investigation; she wanted to leave, but Detective Price had asked them to stay until they had finished their preliminary interviews. Her interview hadn't gone well. From the moment she entered the back office, it was like she was in a tunnel, and all she could think about was murder and the possibility that one of them might be arrested. Mari knew that Detective Price was just doing his job, but she resented his intrusive questions about Steve's private life, about their relationship with each other, about her father. Again and again, the conversation had returned to her father.

When she came out of the restroom shortly after the interview ended, Detective Price and his colleague Officer Penny were standing near the door still talking about him.

"It's too soon to make an arrest," said the detective. "But we may have a suspect. We can verify that José, his daughter, and Mateo the bus boy were all in the restaurant at the time of the murder. And while Marisol Ramirez and Mateo were apparently together, no one can verify the whereabouts of Mr. Ramirez."

"You don't think he was in his office?" Officer Penny asked.

"He may have been," Detective Price said quietly. "He says he was. They say he was, but we don't know. It won't be enough to convict him in court, but it is a lead. The only other possibility is that he was attacked by a fourth person that the three of them did not know was in the restaurant."

Mari did not think her anger could burn any brighter, but then Officer Penny said, "I don't think we should be so quick to rule out Mari and Mateo. We've seen this kind of murder before, where two people give each other an airtight alibi at the time of the crime, but it turns out that they were both guilty."

"I thought of that," Detective Price responded. "And I'm not trying to discount it, but it's hard to look at those two and think they could be that clever." He paused for a moment before adding, "Plus, while Mari was obviously not enamored of the victim, she doesn't strike me as harboring any particular hostility toward him."

"But we've seen that before, too," Officer Penny replied, who Mari desperately wished would stop talking. "Maybe she doesn't appear suspicious at the moment because she took all her anger out on Steve Wilson?"

***

Later that night in her apartment, Mari warmed up some shrimp tostadas and paced the kitchen trying to sort out what she knew.

Two things had struck her as suspicious. First, Mateo had shown up to work early. And second, Alex and David had shown up late. Mari didn't for a moment think that her brothers had been involved in the murder—they hadn't even been at the restaurant, as far as she knew—but she needed to know where they had been. The fact that Mari's brothers had been so evasive when she had asked them about their whereabouts only confirmed that they were up to something sketchy.

Mari gave Tabasco the remains of her meal and sank into the couch. A colorful blanket decorated with red, blue, and green patterns lay draped over it. Mari pulled the colorful blanket over her tired body. Now that the passions of the moment had subsided, she could admit to herself that she didn't know where her dad had been at the time of the murder. It was an unpleasant fact of the case that Mari didn't want to think about, but she had to.

She had to clear her family's name.

José Ramirez was an unlikely suspect. The only person he really hated was Mr. Chun across the street. If Mari's father were going to murder anyone, it would have been him. The whole town knew that. Honestly, there weren't any likely suspects. Nobody hated Steve Wilson enough to want him dead. No one particularly thought about Steve at all. He was just there, like the elms in Birchwood Park. Steve had been a fixture in the community for as long as anyone could remember, pleasantly smiling and bland, not especially threatening or intelligent. Just there.

Steve had no family in town, but he must have had family somewhere. Mari would start there. She would find out where his parents lived if they were still living and contact them. Mari would talk to Steve's siblings if he had any. Maybe finding out his family history would illuminate his unfortunate end.

And, just because it was bothering her so much, Mari would talk to her brothers. She picked up her cell phone to call them when the phone began ringing. It was Mari's father.

"Hola, dad," said Mari answered.

"I know you don't have plans tonight, so don't say you do," Mr. Ramirez responded. "I need you to get back here."

"Back to the restaurant?"

"We're opening for dinner," he clarified. "Be here in fifteen minutes."

"Dad, are you even allowed to be opening?" Mari questioned. "Did the police say you could do this?"

There was no answer because José Ramirez had already hung up.

CHAPTER FOUR

Mari's prediction from that morning had proven correct. Lito Bueno's Mexican Restaurant was seeing its best business in years. When she pulled up to the restaurant ten minutes after getting off of the phone with her dad, a group of teenagers was playing hacky sack in the last open parking space. Mari yelled at them to move, even threatening to run over them, but they remained fixed.

Not wanting to cause a scene, Mari drove across the street to the Lucky Noodle, whose parking lot was also beginning to fill up. The restaurant itself, however, was virtually empty. Whole families were abandoning their cars and dashing back across the street to Lito Bueno's Mexican Restaurant. Mr. Chun stared enviously through the slatted blinds of his Chinese restaurant at the long line that snaked its way out of the dark lobby and halfway around the building.

Ignoring the flashes of the photographers and the shouts of customers who thought she was cutting in line, Mari cut her way through the crowd, past the foyer, and into the kitchen. There she found Alex and David washing pans. Her brothers had been given the least glamorous of jobs and would be working late to make up for the hours they had missed that morning. Chrissy Davenport, the sprightly young waitress, blonde and bubbly, was just beginning her shift. She hadn't known about the murder until Mr. Ramirez had called her into his office. Chrissy hadn't had a chance to talk about it with anyone else, and so spent several minutes questioning Mari about the discovery of the body and her subsequent interrogation.

"Like, what did they ask you?" Chrissy said, who seemed to find the whole thing wonderfully thrilling. "Did it feel like you were being treated as a suspect?"

"They wanted to know where I was and who I was with when it happened, really basic stuff," Mari replied. "I didn't have much to say. I just explained to them that I had been hanging out back with Mateo until Tabasco started barking, and would not stop. I came out here to get him, and you know the rest." Mari found she didn't want to dwell on the unsavory details that would undoubtedly be endlessly repeated in the newspapers and local gossip.

"You brave soul, you must have been so scared, finding the body like that," Chrissy commented. "I can't believe…" She glanced around to make sure no one could hear her, and then leaned forward and whispered, "I can't believe you're working tonight after what you went through today."

"Neither can I," Mari said with a shrug. "But that's life. The world doesn't stop just because someone dies, you know?"

"You're so brave," Chrissy said again, shaking her head in wonder. "Your true love was killed, practically in front of you."

"We weren't lovers." Mari rolled her eyes. "And I didn't see anything. You're being a bit dramatic."

"He was smitten with you," Chrissy went on, seeming not to hear her. "It's going to be strange not seeing his meat truck driving through town every day."

Mari was relieved when the doors to the restaurant opened and Chrissy no longer had the time speculate about Mari's love life. The table where Steve had been sitting that morning had been roped off, and a sign placed near it asking customers not to go near it. So, of course, children and even a few adults had tiptoed over the rope and had touched the once blood-stained chair as though it was a holy relic. Mari felt it would have made more sense to hide the chair and then rope off a completely different table, pretending it was the scene of the crime. Customers would have the grim pleasure of thinking they were sitting at the victim's table, and her dad wouldn't have to come out every few minutes and shoo them away, looking more and more grumpy each time.

About a hundred people were seated in the dining room at one time, while another hundred waited in the lobby or stood in line outside. For a while, Chrissy busily sat people on the long Spanish-style benches by the front doors as they waited for the line to move forward. Eventually, Chrissy ran out of spaces and instead began urging the crowd, in the loudest and sternest voice she could muster, to leave the seats available for the pregnant and elderly.

Of course, there was one man who couldn't be bothered to stand in line. Mr. Chun from the

Lucky Noodle strode in from across the street and, ignoring the cries and protests of waiting customers, planted himself at the front of the line and demanded a seat.

"I'm very sorry," Chrissy patiently said, who was so taken aback by this presumptuous gesture that she didn't know how to respond. "I'm afraid you'll have to wait in line like everyone else."

"This is ridiculous," Mr. Chun replied, a single vein in the middle of his forehead throbbing dangerously. "If I wait, it will take at least an hour to be seated."

"Two hours," said Chrissy.

"I want a table and I want it now."

Chrissy assured Mr. Chun that she would see what she could do. A few minutes later, she returned wearing a sober expression, her lips pursed into a frown.

"I've spoken to the manager," Chrissy said. "I'm afraid we won't be able to seat you at all tonight."

"This is ridiculous," Mr. Chun shouted, slamming his fist down hard on the wooden podium. Chrissy and several customers jumped. "This is an outrage!"

"I'm sorry, those are my orders," said Chrissy. Then, addressing the crowd, she said in a loud voice, "I've been asked to let you know that only those who are currently inside the building will be seated tonight. The rest of you will have to return tomorrow." Turning back to Mr. Chun, she said in a faint voice, "That includes you, Sir."

"But I am inside the building!" Mr. Chun yelled, nearly exploding with rage. "What kind of madness is this?"

"You weren't in line," Chrissy reminded him, her voice becoming so quiet with each new outburst that by now it was scarcely audible.

Taking a deep breath, she said, "Only those who were inside the building, *and in line*, will be seated. We apologize for the inconvenience, but there just isn't enough room."

"Let me talk to your manager," Mr. Chun demanded, and pushed past Chrissy before she could stop him. But at that moment José Ramirez came striding out of his office, his sleeves rolled up as though he was getting ready for a fight.

"I demand an apology for my mistreatment," Mr. Chun said to Mr. Ramirez. Families at all tables turned to look at the two headstrong men. "I demand an apology and your famous churro deluxe platter."

"You'll never get it," José snidely answered. "You'd love that recipe, wouldn't you? You've spent spies into my restaurant one too many times to steal my recipes. How dare you come in here and demand a seat at one of my tables. Don't you have any of your own customers to feed?"

"You apologize now, or I'll tell all of these nice people about the time you had mice in your kitchen," Mr. Chun threatened.

"*You* were the one who put them there!" José shouted in response, his cheeks turning bright red.

"You can't prove that!" Mr. Chun placed his hands on his hips.

"But I sure as habanero can kick you out of my restaurant!" José attempted to yell his response even louder.

By now silence had fallen over the whole room, unbroken even by the sounds of cutlery hitting plates. Turning to face the diners, Mr. Chun pointed one menacing finger into the air and said, "I'm amazed at all of you, eating so cheerfully when a murder was committed in this very room not twelve hours ago. Someone answer me this question: why were the police parked outside all morning? Is it because they suspect that someone who works at this rest—"

But Mr. Chun never finished the question. A quick blow to the face sent him spiraling to the floor. Alarmed, Mari and Mateo ran Mr. Ramirez, grabbing his arms as he lunged forward.

"Dad, it's not worth it," Mari said. "You really will go to jail."

"I don't care," her dad snarled. "I've been putting up with this for too many years."

Paula Ramirez, Mari's mother, came running to the front of the restaurant. It was the first time Mari had seen her since Steve's murder. Giving her husband a scolding look, she glared at the two men.

"Let me deal with this, Mari," Paula muttered. She turned to Mr. Chun. "Get out of here before I call the police."

"That's right," Mr. Ramirez added, "and—"

"Not so fast, José," Paula cut in. "You should be ashamed of yourself punching people in the middle of our restaurant. Both of you quit acting like children." Paula nodded, matter-of-factly.

If anyone had reason to call the police, Mari reflected, it was Mr. Chun. But he was too busy rubbing his jaw and making sure all his teeth were still in place to bother with legalities. Mari's mom was the one person he had never been able to argue with. Mari had often wondered if he secretly had a thing for her.

"Leave before this escalates any further," Paula said again.

With slumped shoulders, Mr. Ramirez turned and walked back to his office. Mr. Chun folded his arms as he watched his opponent leave in surrender.

"This isn't over, José," Mr. Chun mumbled angrily.

"Ay dios mio, Mr. Chun," Paula responded, shooing him away. "Don't be such a Peking Duck."

CHAPTER FIVE

By the next morning, Lito Bueno's Mexican Restaurant had gone somewhat back to normal. The police had shown up shortly after Mr. Chun had walked out of the restaurant the night before, and had spent another hour interviewing him and Mr. Ramirez separately. Mari heard from Chrissy, who had heard it from her roommate who had briefly dated Mr. Chun's daughter the year before, that Mr. Chun had declined to press charges.

Mari spent the morning dealing with the continued fallout from Steve Wilson's death. The fact that the only meat-deliverer in town had been killed meant that there was no longer anyone in town to order meat from. The three people Mari had called from neighboring towns had seemed interested in expanding their businesses until they learned that the previous man who had held the job title had been murdered. After that, most of Mari's prospects had regretfully said that they were already over-booked, that gasoline prices were too high, etc., etc.

Mari had some time to figure out a solution. There was enough meat in the freezer to last them a couple of days. But soon they would have to find another means of delivery. The whole town would, or they'd be serving nothing but salads from dawn to dusk. And if there was one thing Mari's dad was adamant about, it was that Lito Bueno's Mexican Restaurant never had and never would serve salad. He had called that dish *chicken feed* for as long as Mari could remember. And Mr. Ramirez had insisted that his restaurant didn't serve chicken feed.

When Mateo came in at noon, looking as groggy as ever, Mari placed him on the phone looking for a new meat supplier and turned her attention to questioning her brothers.

"We've been down this road before," Mari said. "I'm not giving up until I get a straight answer out of you. I just want to know what you two were doing yesterday during the *two hours* you weren't here. Come on, take this seriously. A man is dead."

"We were studying for our calculus final," David answered, while Alex gave an entirely different answer.

When Mari continued to glare at them, Alex said that they had gone to a movie while David had insisted, at the same time, that the two of them were volunteering at the hospital.

"That's the most absurd thing you've said so far," Mari responded to David as Tabasco growled behind them. "Don't try to convince me you've suddenly decided to be charitable. You were both up to no good, or you wouldn't be lying right now."

"Sorry," Alex said, "but we can't tell you what we've been up to. All you need to know is that we had nothing to do with what happened to Steve."

Mari bit her tongue in frustration. "I don't think you realize how serious this is. You were out goofing off when a man was killed, and he wouldn't have been killed if you weren't out goofing off. And now, thanks to your negligence, Dad might go to prison." Mari observed her brothers as their faces went white. "You didn't hear what I heard yesterday. Those officers think Dad killed Steve Wilson. They think he walked in here and stabbed him in the back. They want to make an arrest, but they're still gathering evidence."

"But if they don't find any evidence..." David started.

"... which they won't," Alex finished, "because Dad did not kill Steve Wilson."

"That's not the point," Mari nearly shouted. "Dad is under heavy suspicion. And until that cloud of suspicion lifts off of him, things are going to be very hard for all of us. The town is going to think we're protecting him. We're going to lose friends and customers, and money. We could go out of business! And none of this would have happened if you two had been here."

***

Realizing she needed to calm down before she punched one or both of her brothers in the face, Mari spent the rest of the morning making tortillas with her Abuela. Mari's grandmother was a tiny woman who only spoke Spanish and could often be heard muttering with fierce disapproval to anyone who would listen.

The tortilla-making process was involved but not especially difficult with practice. Mari's Abuela kneaded a mixture of flour and salt, occasionally adding water until it was smooth all over. Because she didn't like to rush, this normally took about twenty minutes with each batch. Once the mixture had been allowed to rest for another ten minutes, Mari pressed the dough into several, thin, circular shapes. Mari then fried the tortillas. An hour later, a nice pile of tortillas accumulated on a plate at the edge of the stove.

Flipping tortillas wasn't especially labor-intensive, so Mari had ample time to reflect on the events of the last couple of days. She seemed to have spooked her brothers with her talk of Dad going to jail. It was unlikely they would cave in immediately, but she had persuaded them that she was thinking only of the good of the family. Whatever their faults, Mari's brothers loved their family. Maybe in a few days one or both of them would tell her what was going on.

Mari hoped Alex and David hadn't been up to any serious mischief. But until her brothers were up-front with her about where they'd been, Mari wouldn't be able to trust them. Trust was essential if Mari wanted to succeed at saving her family's reputation. Mari needed to unite the whole family in this endeavor, but that was impossible as long as certain members of the family were keeping secrets from each other.

Mari paused as she realized she had let one tortilla cook for too long on one side. It had browned too much, and she would have to throw it out. That's how things were, lately. She was having trouble focusing on the day-to-day needs of the restaurant because her quest to find the killer had become all-consuming. Mari knew that her father would be devastated if anything happened to the family restaurant. In fact, the entire family would have a hard time coping. Lito Bueno's Mexican Restaurant represented a lifetime of hard work and life savings. Mari had to figure out what happened to Steve Wilson before things took a turn for the worst.

Mari picked up the plate of tortillas and set it down next to her Abuela. She was dimly conscious that people were arguing all around her. Faintly, as though from a great distance, she heard her father complaining about Tabasco being in the restaurant again. Her Abuela was telling him in Spanish that a pair of her shoes had gone missing. Mari's grandmother seemed to think it was very important that they knew this. She thought it might be connected to the mystery of who had killed Steve Wilson.

There were times when the demands of the restaurant and being surrounded by so many people got to be too much, and this was one of those times. Mari needed to shut herself in the bathroom and think. If she did enough thinking, maybe she could figure this out on her own. Mari excused herself in a faint voice and left the kitchen.

But even before she had reached the door of the women's restroom, another mystery presented itself. Someone had left the back door of the restaurant wide open.

CHAPTER SIX

Mari feared that she was losing her mind. Surely an open door at the back of a restaurant wasn't cause for concern. In ordinary times it wouldn't have been, but there had been nothing ordinary about this week.

Mari stumbled into the bathroom, feeling like she might puke at any moment. Someone was trying to sabotage the restaurant. Someone was trying to hurt her family. It could be someone who worked at the restaurant. It could be someone she knew.

Panic fought with reason, with panic seizing the upper hand. Trust was the quality Mari valued most in other people. It was the reason she hadn't been in a relationship for longer than a year after college because each of her boyfriends had violated that sacred trust in one way or another. Only the members of her immediate family merited that kind of trust. If she couldn't trust them, she couldn't trust anyone.

Mari was slightly jumpy for the rest of the day. Whenever her dad called her name—when he informed her that he was locking Tabasco in the office where he would be less of a nuisance—she twitched uncomfortably. It was hard for Mari to conceal the fact that she was feeling uneasy about everyone who worked in the restaurant. She was quite sure they could see through her and knew the concerns that were pouring through her head. Mari tried to take deep breaths to control her anxiety.

It was past midnight when Mari's dad left for home after escorting out the last customers. Mari was left to lock up the restaurant on her own. Because Mateo had already begun cleaning the dining room about half an hour before closing, there wasn't much tidying up to do. She did, however, have to sanitize the soda fountains to prevent grime from accumulating. Too much of it attracted insects which were a common problem in Texas during the spring and summer months.

Mari walked into the dining room one final time to make sure everything was in order before she turned out the lights. The room looked spooky at this time of night, with all the wooden chairs stacked neatly on the red tabletops. Light filtered in through the window from the single street lamp that illuminated the road running between Lito Bueno's Mexican Restaurant and the Lucky Noodle. Across the street, Mr. Chun was just closing his blinds. He paused for a second, seeming to glare from across the street as if sensing that Mari was watching him.

Walking back toward the kitchen, Mari heard a scuttling noise and a small shape darted past her. She jumped. It was either a rat or a cockroach, though the thought of either creature sneaking around the restaurant made her want to vomit. She closed her eyes, not wanting to see find out. But somehow that made it even more frightening.

Suddenly there was a crash and a rattle from the kitchen. Mari found herself halfway to the back door before she even knew where she was. *Was* it a rat? As bad as that would be, every alternative was worse. A man had been murdered in the restaurant, and now she was hearing strange noises in the middle of the night. Something, or someone, was crashing around back there. By a sheer act of will, Mari tiptoed toward the kitchen and grabbed the biggest steak knife she could find.

No one was in there—or at least no one she could see. If there had been anyone, Mari reasoned, they almost certainly would have attacked her when she'd had her back turned. Somehow that thought did not fill her with comfort.

Mari made her way to the back door, through which the family left every night after locking up. It was open again. Seeing it open flooded her with mixed emotions. Maybe the back door was always open, and she'd never noticed until this week. Heat flushed into her face as she laughed at her own silly conclusions. And yet there had been the noises, and the constant feeling like she was being watched, like someone, was hovering right behind her.

A commotion came from the front of the building. There was more scuffling and even shouting. The cadence of the voices was familiar. It was Mari's two brothers. She closed the back door and made her way back through the dining room to the front doors.

Police lights flashed into the windows. Two officers escorted David and Alex to the front of the restaurant. David was busy explaining how their parents had already gone home for the night and there was no way they could get in when Mari disabled the alarm and came walking out.

"What have you got for me tonight, officers?" Mari said, disappointed.

"Don't mean to disturb you, Ms. Ramirez," said the taller of the two officers. "We found these two boys street-racing out near the train tracks."

"Illegally," added the second officer, as if this needed to be said. "They're lucky they're not in jail, but I figure the family's got enough goin' on right now."

"Thanks, fellas," Mari said in a friendly voice. "I'll take care of these two." As the policemen returned to their cars, Mari glared at the two boys with a stern expression.

"We know what you're going to say," Alex said first.

"So, there's really no need to say anything," David added.

"Then we'll cut right to the chase," Mari replied. "I want you to tell me what's stopping me from going straight to Mom and Dad and telling them why you weren't at work yesterday."

"For one, because you love us," Alex answered with a mischievous grin. "And I, for one, know you would deeply regret it if anything terrible happened to us."

"You would cry into your pillow every night," David added. "You'd regret it to the end of your days."

"You still haven't given me a reason." Mari shook her head.

"Because it's the right thing to do?" suggested Alex. "Because one Ramirez never rats out another Ramirez? How many more reasons do you need?"

"And if I choose not to tell Mom and Dad what I know," Mari continued, "what do I get in return?"

"Our undying love." Alex gratefully held out his arms.

"Hmm, not good enough," Mari replied.

"We will never take cash out of your wallet again," David commented.

"Unlikely."

"I'm all out of ideas." David threw his hands in the air. "Why don't you stop torturing us and tell us what you want?"

"Just this," Mari said, and her eyes burned with a fierce glow. "I won't tell our parents what the two of you have been up to if you'll agree to help me catch a murderer…for the restaurant's sake."

CHAPTER SEVEN

That night Mari slept fitfully. She dreamt that she was back at the restaurant, helping Tabasco make a Delicioso Special. Somehow Tabasco was a full-sized person, and he sounded just like a New Yorker. He was what Tabasco might have looked like if he had been human, but with his combination of combativeness and cheerfulness. The two were talking and working together like old friends. Tabasco, who turned out to be an expert at making cakes, made the dulce de leche cake and the chocolate chili cake while Mari made deep-fried vanilla ice cream.

Mari woke briefly and got out of bed to get a glass of water, and when she fell back asleep, the dream had taken a different turn. Her dad had figured out that Tabasco was helping Mari make desserts and had forbidden him from ever coming back into the restaurant. "I don't want to see him in here with his dog hands," Mari's father had said in her dream. "He's a dog a murderer!"

And suddenly Detective Price and Officer Penny marched Tabasco to prison, surrounded by the flashing lights of reporters who wanted to know how Mari could have sheltered and defended a killer.

Mari awoke suddenly at 8:00 AM to the sound of Tabasco's barking. Someone was knocking on the door. Mari remembered that her brothers had said they would be coming over in the morning, though they hadn't said why. She had forgotten to set the alarm. Shouting apologies, Mari stumbled into a pair of blue jeans and raced into the living room.

"Where are we going?" Mari said, dazed and still sleepy. "What's going on?"

"You'll just have to see," David and Alex responded in unison. As though in a dream Mari drifted down the stairs after them. They drove through the town square, past their dad's restaurant, past the railroad tracks into the abandoned industrial part of town. Not too long ago red smokestacks had belched smoke into the air day and night, and the noise of trains coming and going was omnipresent. Now, the smokestacks were rusting ruins against the blue summer sky.

David turned into the empty parking lot of a shopping center littered with discarded bottles and free-floating trash bags. In front of them stood rows of old storefronts with boarded-up windows. It was an abandoned shopping center.

"You see that place?" David said, pointing to the edge of a building. "That's where we're going."

Mari wanted to ask how he expected to get in but realized that the honest answer was probably one she didn't want to hear.

She was right.

As the three siblings approached a wooden door—rough and unpainted, like a block of wood in a carpenter's shop—David instructed Alex to ensure no one was watching them. Alex strode back to the edge of the concrete and placed his hand over his eyes in the most conspicuous way, like a sailor gazing out over the far horizon. He looked to left and right.

"We're the only people in this parking lot," Alex announced.

"What about over there?" said Mari, pointing at the opposite end of the shopping center.

"Over there?" Alex responded. "No one will see us."

"Okay, but how are we going to get in?" Mari asked.

"Today, Mari," David answered, "you're going to learn that sometimes having brothers who are willing to bend the rules a little has its advantages." Pulling out a credit card, he held it up in front of her.

"Do I even want to know what you're about to do?" Mari asked.

"Well, I would hate for you to turn me in so...no." Deftly and gently, Alex took the card and slipped it in between the lock and the door frame. With a satisfying click, the lock gave way and the door opened.

Mari gaped at him. "How many buildings are you able to break into with that trick?"

"See, I told you she wouldn't be able to handle it," David commented. "She's too much of a goody-goody."

"If *goody-goody* is your definition of a responsible adult," Mari added.

"Relax, you asked for help, and that's what we're giving you," Alex said, ushering them both inside. "Now hurry up and shut the door before we're all in trouble."

"What is this place?" Mari glanced around at the unkempt room.

"This was Steve's office," David answered.

Mari stood in the doorway, hesitating. If she followed them inside and they were caught, the whole family would be in trouble. That would have looked horrible on the news. The incident could be spun very badly. And even if they weren't caught, Mari's brothers might think she was condoning their actions by following them inside. Not to mention, that her father would have a heart attack if he knew what they were doing.

"Come on, Mari," David said, who seemed to sense her reservations. "You said you wanted to help Dad out. This is how we're going to do it."

Ignoring the anxiety that was twisting at her insides, Mari crossed over the threshold into the cool silence of Steve's office.

One corner of the room looked like a normal office, though one that was uniquely cluttered. Papers lay scattered everywhere. A bowl of dry cat food stood half-empty on the desk, and a small tower of tax documents threatened to topple over at any moment. The freezer room where Steve's meat was stored was right next to his desk. Anyone sitting in Steve's swivel chair could easily see most of the room.

Alex stood in the doorway quietly scanning the street for signs of cars while David and Mari examined the stacks of papers on top of the desk.

"We could be here for hours," Mari commented, noting the differences between her father's organized file folders and Steve's piles of mess. "I've never seen anyone so disorganized."

"Here are some newspaper clippings," David said. "Hey here's one from when you gave that interview when the restaurant was doing that charity thing."

"Why is there a newspaper clipping of me?" Mari bit her lip.

"That's not the only one," David continued. "Listen to this. *Hometown Heroine Returns from College. Local Restaurateur Has Thoughts on the Presidential Electoin*, and *Election* is spelled wrong. Nice."

"Someone at the newspaper has a thing for you," Alex concluded.

"And it looks like they're not the only one," David added. "Steve had an entire portfolio of clippings."

"I've got an idea," Alex said, scratching his chin. "Maybe Steve was a serial killer, and whoever killed him was doing the community a favor."

"He was doing *Mari* a favor, from the looks of it," David replied.

"Will you guys cut it out?" Mari, who wanted to disappear under the covers, kept a brave face. "We need to stay focused. If we can find Steve's delivery route schedule, we'll know all the businesses in town he delivered to the day he died. We can begin drawing up a list of possible suspects. People he knew, enemies he might have made."

"There are about a dozen open bank statements." David observed Steve's desk, brushing aside a key ring with a dozen keys on it. He held up one of the papers and flipped it over. "It looks like he was in some serious financial trouble."

Mari took the statement and scanned it. "He couldn't afford the upkeep for this office. The bank was getting ready to foreclose, which would have been the end of his business. This is the first serious piece of evidence we have." Mari gathered up the bank statements and placed them in her purse.

"You'd think the police would've inspected this place before they started making accusations against Dad," Alex commented. "What are they going to do when they get here and find all his important files missing?"

"They won't know what is or isn't missing," Mari said absently. She held up a yellow spreadsheet, flipping it over as though to make sure it was real. "Here's his delivery route."

David came over to get a closer look at it, but Alex said, "Okay, a truck has been circling the parking lot for the last couple of minutes."

"What was the last stop on his route, before the restaurant?" David asked, who didn't seem to have heard Alex.

"The Lucky Noodle," Mari answered with an air of triumph. "That's our next stop."

"Okay, but I really think we need to get out of here," Alex reminded them. "I seriously can't stress enough how sketchy this truck is being."

David and Mari both went to the door and peeked outside. A black pickup truck made circles around the parking lot. Only one person was in the vehicle, a bearded man in his late fifties wearing a camo vest.

"Maybe I'm overreacting, but…" Alex shrugged.

"Maybe you are," Mari responded. "But I don't want to stick around and find out. David, grab the spreadsheet and let's go."

David grabbed the spreadsheet off of the top of the pile. Unbeknownst to Mari, he also grabbed Steve's keys and hastily stuffed them into the side pockets of his cargo pants.

CHAPTER EIGHT

The next morning, Mari and her brothers stood outside the front door of the Lucky Noodle at 8:00 AM. The dining room lights were on, indicating that someone was inside. The chairs had been carefully unstacked and arranged around their respective tables. The floor looked as though it had been newly mopped, and a yellow mop bucket stood next to the podium where the hostess greeted customers. As loudly as Mari knocked, no one answered.

"You're not pounding hard enough," David said, pushing Mari aside and slamming his fists on the red wooden door with the faux-golden handles. "Open up! It's the police!"

"David, don't say that," Mari scolded him, glancing around to make sure no one had heard them. "Impersonating an officer is against the law."

"You have no room to talk after what we just did," Alex replied. Mari rolled her eyes. The silhouette of a curly-haired figure darted for a split-second out of the kitchen. "It looks like someone heard us."

"Hey, I saw you," David shouted, pounding as hard as ever. "Open up!" Mari placed both hands on his arm to calm him down. "I know you're in there, Jia. Don't fear my good looks. Come on!

"You're such a jerk sometimes, I swear," Mari muttered.

"Yes, but he has a point." Alex shrugged. "Jia's a real--"

"Watch your language," Mari cut in.

Jia Chun was Mr. Chun's daughter and the restaurant's manager. She occupied roughly the same position in the business as Mari did. They had gone to school together and graduated in the same year. For years Jia had liked Evan, the boy Mari ended up dating and the boy she had briefly been engaged to once. When Mari went away to college, Jia had stayed behind to help her father. Jia saw it as her duty as his eldest daughter.

The three Ramirez siblings fell silent. A second light had turned on in the restaurant, and the curly-headed figure strutted toward them. A moment later the door had been unlocked, and Jia Chun was staring back at them, blinking back sunlight.

"My dad really can't know we're talking right now," Jia stated. "But I also don't want the whole neighborhood to hear you. Just come in."

"See," David said to Mari. "Sometimes you have to be a jerk to get what you want."

"What do you want?" Jia turned and walked back into the cool restaurant with its glowing aquariums lining the paneled walls. The three siblings followed without question. There was little expression on Jia's face.

Mari expected Jia to lead them into their office because that was where she and the rest of her family held their private meetings. But Jia paused at the edge of the dining room. Mari looked around. She'd only been inside the Lucky Noodle a few times for obvious reasons.

"Alright, make it quick," said Jia said with a slight roll of her eyes.

"We want to know about Steve Wilson," Mari began.

"Steve Wilson?" Jia replied. "What about him?"

"We know he came to your restaurant just before he was killed." Mari paused for a moment.

"And, might I add, he was killed in *your* restaurant." Jia folded her arms. "You should go looking for answers there and leave the Lucky Noodle out of it."

David stepped forward. "Now wait just a minute."

"Let me handle this, okay?" Mari said to her brother. Mari turned to Jia. "The more you cooperate, the sooner we'll be out of here. Like you said, you wouldn't want your dad to find out we've been talking. Does that sound fair?"

Jia sighed and pulled a cigarette out of her shirt pocket. Mari's eyes went wide. But Jia didn't light her cigarette. Instead, she put it in her mouth and let it dangle there while she talked as if it made the stress of being interrogated by a Ramirez more manageable.

"I don't know what to tell you," Jia responded. "Steve came in yesterday morning and stocked the freezers like he always does on Mondays. I guess he looked more nervous than usual, but that could be because he was sweating. It was hot outside. Nothing new."

"I remember." Mari nodded.

"Steve said hi to my dad, and he was in a good mood. Which I actually did find odd. Steve is never in a good mood." Jia shrugged. "I don't know. I just figured he'd gotten lucky the night before or something."

"Yeah, I guess that is a little strange," Mari replied.

"What," David interrupted. "That Steve got lucky?" His brother Alex chuckled.

"No, that he wasn't his usual depressing self," Jia said without so much a half-smile. "I don't know why you're all so surprised. I've sensed this misfortune for years. He always ordered the number four special, and Dad always says that number four is an unlucky number."

Mari told Jia what she knew about the bank wanting to foreclose on Steve's business, though she was careful to omit how she had found this out. Jia narrowed her eyes, as though wondering how Mari had acquired this vital piece of information.

"Well, there you go," Jia said. "That pretty much settles it. Bankruptcy is like a death sentence. It's not something you can run from. When it happens, it destroys you. I guess Steve saw it coming and decided to take matters into his own hands."

"That doesn't explain how he was found with a knife in his back," Mari replied. "I don't know if you've ever tried to stab yourself in the back but I can't imagine that it's easy."

"He could've hired someone?" Jia suggested. "It could happen. People do really weird things sometimes."

"You think Steve hired someone to murder him because he was going bankrupt?" Mari said. "That's ridiculous." At that moment a young man with a thin goatee came barreling out of the kitchen at top speed and nearly ran her over. He carried a plastic container filled with silverware that clinked and rattled as he walked.

"Excuse me." Mari rubbed her arm where he had bumped into it. "I don't think we've met."

The young man rolled his eyes just as Jia had done earlier. He gave Mari a bold look as if blaming her for being in his way. He then mumbled a few words in Chinese and trotted off.

"My cousin," Jia explained. "He's here from China helping us out during the summer, but he hardly does anything. Of course, my dad won't hear any arguments. To him he's family, and that's all that matters."

"I get it," Mari confessed, glancing at her brothers as they whispered to one another.

Jia escorted them all to the exit. "Time's up."

"Yeah." Mari sighed and followed her brothers into the parking lot. She shook her head at Alex and David. "Did you two really have to have a side conversation while I was trying to talk to Jia?"

"Mari, I've seen Jia's cousin before," David responded. "His name is Desh."

"Where have you seen him?" Mari asked.

"Street racing," David answered.

CHAPTER NINE

When they were safely seated again in a corner booth of their own restaurant, Mari, Alex, and David discussed what they had learned over sopapillas and vanilla ice cream.

"I think Jia did it," Alex joked. "She has a pretty dry personality."

"Alex, be serious," Mari responded. "Jia didn't hate Steve. She hardly knew him."

"She *does* hate you, though," David said. "Maybe she killed him to get back at you."

"That makes absolutely no sense, David." Mari wrinkled her nose.

"Yeah, David," Alex added with a chuckle.

"I still think it was Jia," David said, dipping one corner of his sopapilla into a bowl of half-melted ice cream. "She's the sneaky type. She could have been in here and out without anyone noticing. I mean, she does work right across the street."

"No one cares about your bogus theories," Alex chimed in.

"Sure they do," David argued. "Besides, I haven't heard any better ones from you two." David grabbed one of Mari's sopapillas. "Think about it. What better way to get even with your number one nemesis than to frame her for murder? I wouldn't put it past the Chuns."

"Win, win, win," Alex responded.

David waved a fork at him. "Exactly."

"No offense, but that seems a little far-fetched. Jia's petty, but she doesn't strike me as murderous. And if she wanted to get revenge or whatever, there are better ways to do it than by randomly killing someone and hoping the murder gets pinned on a Ramirez." Mari sighed.

"I'm not saying this was planned," David went on. "I'm saying that Jia saw the opportunity and she took it. No one would suspect her."

"Sorry, I'm still not buying it," Mari argued. "You're forgetting a huge piece of the puzzle. Steve's business was failing. Who stood to gain by Steve being gone? Or who would have also been affected by a bankruptcy? That's what we've got to look out for."

"Or maybe Steve borrowed money from the wrong people to keep himself afloat?" David answered. "Maybe someone came collecting, and Steve couldn't pay up?"

"Yeah," Alex added, "like the mafia."

Mari rubbed her forehead. "Here's what we're going to do tonight. I want you to talk to everyone who comes in tonight. Ask them questions, but don't be weird about it. Just keep the conversation focused on Steve, and watch how people react."

"So, you think I'm onto to something?" Alex asked. "Do you think there's a mob boss in town?"

Mari couldn't believe that Alex's theory was the best one she'd heard all day. Steve definitely needed the money and judging from the papers on his desk, he wasn't the sort of person a bank would have taken a chance on.

"Maybe." Mari took a deep breath and braced herself for the rush of customers that would soon be filling the restaurant.

***

Mari waited tables along with her two brothers because business was still booming and the restaurant was under-staffed. Two hundred people showed up when Lito Bueno's Mexican Restaurant had opened for dinner, and Mari had to turn away fifty. She'd handed out vouchers for a complimentary dessert to the disappointed bunch.

But a portion of customers, sour about being turned away, walked across the street to the Lucky Noodle. Mari decided to keep this information to herself for the time being. Her father was stressed enough with the police breathing down his back.

Mari tried not to let the occasional complaint get to her. She had been in the restaurant business long enough to know that getting criticized was a job hazard. She took her mind off of it by concentrating on the remaining customers and subtly grilling them about Steve Wilson. Although she had been disgusted by their fascination with the crime, now Mari exploited it with the air of a showman.

"This is the chair where it happened," Mari said, motioning to a random chair about fifty feet away from where it had happened. "It took us hours to clean everything."

"Can I touch it?" asked a small tousle-headed boy.

"No, Brian," his mother said, hitting him lightly on the arm. She eagerly looked at Mari. "Can *I* touch it?"

Mari allowed the woman to touch it since it wasn't the actual chair where the murder had taken place. Soon a crowd of people flocked toward Mari's side of the room to hear Mari tell the story of how she had found the body.

"And when I heard the dog's barking," Mari said quietly, "I came running as quick as I could, but it was too late. Steve was dead, and I had been helpless to save him." A single gleaming tear trickled down her cheek. It had started out as a way to draw in the guilty party if the killer had dared set foot in her family's restaurant again. But it had ended with Mari feeling desperate, more than ever, to figure out what had really happened to Steve.

"You poor soul," said an old woman. "You deserve the week off."

"Tell that to my dad," Mari joked, wiping her cheeks. The rest of the room erupted in laughter.

Meanwhile, on the other side of the room, Alex and David were gathered around a table singing *Feliz Cumpleanos* for a family of five. They wore ponchos and sombreros, and the noise they created as they sang made the birthday boy burst into tears. The boy was turning four years old.

Mari met with her brothers as soon as their shift had ended and the last customer had been ushered through the door.

"Did you see that?" Mari said. "Tell me I'm not the only one who saw that. I can't believe he did that."

"Some of us were preoccupied, Mari," David responded. "What did you see?"

"Mateo left work early *again*. He comes in early, and he leaves early. He's not adhering to his schedule at all. I'm going to have to chat with him about it."

"So our next mission," Alex began, who didn't seem overly concerned about Mateo, "is to search the inside of Steve Wilson's house."

Mari bristled with suspicion. "How are we supposed to do that?"

David held up a jingling pair of keys. "The same way we searched his office."

"David Ramirez, where did you get those?" Mari scolded him, with a look that might have shamed a dragon. "Did you swipe them off of Steve's desk? For the love of carnitas, why did you do that? If the police find out, it'll make our family look even worse."

"Chill out, girl." David raised his eyebrows. "No one is going to find out. Besides, you can't just ask us for help and then criticize our methods."

"Yeah, Mari," Alex added. "You know how we roll."

"What am I doing?" Mari muttered to herself. "Alex and David, I want the two of you to put those keys back. We might be investigating a murder, but we are certainly *not* thieves."

CHAPTER TEN

Just as Mari, Alex, and David were getting ready to leave, their dad appeared and demanded that the two boys stay behind to help him with bookkeeping. As usual, Alex and David put up a fight.

"Dad, we had plans tonight," Alex argued.

"You *had* plans," Mr. Ramirez corrected him. "I had plans this week too. Let me tell you about my plans. I had plans to run a business without a nosey detective hovering over my shoulder, but that didn't happen. You two were late the morning of the murder, so you have some time to make up."

"Dad--" Mari interrupted feebly.

"Don't you *dad* me, Marisol. I am sick of people telling me what to do in my own restaurant.

Come on, boys." José walked briskly into his office and slammed the door, sending a framed picture falling off of the wall.

"I think we'd better stay," David said with a heavy sigh. "Sorry, Mari."

"It's okay. I'd hate to see what dad would do if the two of you snuck out anyway." Mari waved goodbye to her brothers and left the restaurant through the back door as she usually did.

Mari understood her father's point of view, even if she thought he'd handled things poorly. She had always been the brightest and hardest-working child in the Ramirez family. José liked to say that Mari had inherited his genes. This is why he'd always pushed her to be the best. David and Alex were a different story, but they were still young. Granted, they were brilliant at other things like street racing and breaking and entering.

José Ramirez would have killed Alex and David if he knew they were street-racing. He saw it as a frivolous waste of time. Anything they had ever shown interest in was a waste of time. It never showed on their faces, but Mari knew her brothers were both hurt by it. And in a weird way, Mari was a little hurt too because she had given up so many of her own interests to help run the restaurant. Mari's one goal in life had been to make her father proud of her. But Mari was never entirely sure how well she had succeeded.

Maybe that was why Mari was so determined to catch the killer. To save the family business, yes, and to exonerate her father's good name. But more than that, Mari wanted her dad to say the words *I'm proud of you* for once. If catching a murderer couldn't get him to do it then maybe nothing ever would.

Mari pulled into the parking lot of the abandoned strip mall she and her brothers had visited. Only a single street lamp cast a thin light over the empty lot, and in some places, there was no light at all. Mari parked directly in front of

Steve's old office and, after a quick scan of the area to make sure she was alone in the shopping center, she crept out of the car.

The only way Mari knew how to get inside was to try the credit card trick David had shown her. She pulled out her debit card and thrust it through the door frame where she assumed the lock was. It opened easily but not because Mari was now a lock-picking expert. The door had already been unlocked.

There was a loud scraping of gravel behind her and Mari instinctively flinched as she turned around. She realized that if a murderer found her out here, there would be little she could do to protect herself. At least Mari's brothers knew where she was, but they were busy at the moment. If anything happened to her, it would be hours before help would arrive.

Suddenly there was another loud *crash* and a hiss that nearly sent Mari scrambling back to her car. Her vision clouded for a second with the thought of all the terrible things that could happen. But when Mari had calmed down a little, she saw two cats nearby growling at each other.

With a loud sigh of relief, Mari walked into the dark office. It would do no good for her to turn the light on, for that would immediately attract the attention of anyone driving by. Instead, she used the light from her cell phone to illuminate her way back to the desk and placed Steve's keys back on top of the pile of bills.

Mari knew she probably should have exited as soon as this task was done, but she couldn't resist poking around a bit longer since she was there. She had nowhere else she needed to be and no one pressuring her to leave. Mari could stay as long as she wanted, provided that no one caught her. She sent a text to David letting him know her plans and prayed their dad didn't read it.

David, of course, was incredulous.

"Mari, get out of there," David texted back.

"Just give me a few minutes," Mari texted him.

"Don't be stupid," was all he wrote in return.

Mari had no idea what she expected to find in the freezers, but she examined them anyway hoping a clue would present itself among the frozen meats. It occurred to her that she could easily walk out with forty pounds of beef. The city was starving for meat ever since Steve's death, and here it all was, right here. But her father would want to know where she'd gotten it, and Mari had *just* finished lecturing her brothers about the importance of not stealing. She breathed a prayer of thanks that the thought of stealing meat hadn't yet occurred to Alex and David.

After looking around for another ten minutes, Mari realized she wasn't going to find anything the police hadn't already found. She began tiptoeing her way towards the entrance.

But as she walked past the front desk, her eyes were struck by a series of framed pictures hanging on the wall. Mari had been so preoccupied the day before, and so afraid of getting caught that she hadn't examined them closely.

Mari held up her phone for a closer look. There was a picture of Steve and his parents when he was quite young. He was wearing Mickey Mouse ears and standing in front of a large castle. Somewhat worryingly, there was a picture of him and her from the day Steve had asked Mari to prom, and she had turned him down. But Mari wasn't the only woman on his wall. Steve had taken pictures of about a dozen different girls from around town.

The last picture in the series must have been taken in his last year of high school. It showed just Steve who was still long-limbed and gawky back then, not the sweaty walrus he became in his later years. He was standing on a stone path, looking rather jaunty in cargo pants, a plain red t-shirt, and a small backpack. Behind him stood a scene of immense beauty, and rolling hills of green to the far horizon. It was as though Steve had wandered into an alternate universe.

An enormous crash sent every nerve in Mari's body on edge. It was like a painting falling or a rat scurrying away. A rat...or something much bigger.

Mari told herself again and again that she had stayed too long. She'd stayed just a minute too long, and now she was going to pay for it.

A shadow appeared in front of the front window. As Mari lowered herself behind Steve's old desk, the hairs on the back of her neck rising, the shadow entered the office and moved toward the center of the room. The mystery figure held a flashlight. Mari couldn't see who it was because she feared revealing her hiding place. She didn't know if the shadow was a friend or a foe.

Every second Mari spent pondering her next course of action was a second wasted. She had little advice for herself because she had never been in this sort of situation. The shadow moved toward the back of the room and examined the frozen meats. Now was Mari's chance to make a run for it. The only alternative was to stay and possibly be caught.

Mari darted up from her hiding spot and ran as fast as she could into the parking lot. Her hands shook, and she had trouble opening her car door. She gulped, hearing the sound of footsteps coming from inside Steve's office.

Finally, Mari unlocked her door and started her engine. But she was a second too late. Just as she was pulling out of her parking spot, a flashlight shined on her face. Mari squinted from the harsh glare.

Mari had no idea who the intruder was, but the intruder now knew who she was.

CHAPTER ELEVEN

Mari sped home as fast as she could, undressed, and climbed into bed. But sleep eluded her that night. She was too worked up and too agitated after the events of the last hour. Someone had caught her breaking into Steve's office. Mari feared what might happen next.

Not all was bad, she reminded herself as she paced the living room with Tabasco at 3:00 AM. Mari had learned some things. For one, it couldn't have been the police breaking into Steve's office which meant there was a murder suspect wandering around town. No one on the police force would have been creeping around like that, and not carrying a warrant. It was either a criminal or another amateur sleuth like herself. Rationally those were the only two possibilities. And if it was a criminal, he couldn't go to the police to report

Mari for trespassing without implicating himself in the process. It wasn't the law Mari had to fear in this instance.

It was something worse.

It was entirely possible that the person who had flashed his or her's flashlight into Mari's face that night as she was pulling away from the office was the person who had murdered Steve Wilson. This person would have no scruples. In Mari's mind, she pictured the killer as a man, terrifying and immense. She wasn't safe anywhere, anymore than Steve had been. If a man could be murdered in a restaurant during the day, then there were few places the arms of the killer could not reach. She might wake up in the middle of the night to find the murderer standing over her, ready to pounce.

Mari sank into the couch and clutched her dog close to her chest. Tabasco let out a resigned whimper. If a murderer got into the apartment, she knew Tabasco wouldn't be much protection. But somehow he made her feel safer. She would be glad when this whole investigation was over, and she could sleep soundly in her bed again.

***

Mari's dad was less than pleased when she brought Tabasco into work the next morning.

"He's not going back outside," Mari protested when her father tried to order the dog back into the car. "It's hot out there, so he'll be staying in here with me. He's not hurting anyone and I'll keep him out of the kitchen."

"And what will my customers think?" Mr. Ramirez asked. "He drools everywhere, he barks at customers, and he's constantly getting into the tabasco supply.

"Well, that is how he earned his name," Mari informed him.

"I've told you time and time again that I don't want him in the restaurant, Mari." José shook his head in disapproval. "Why don't you listen? Why don't any of my children listen to me?"

"I am listening," Mari said. "I just don't agree. And Tabasco doesn't bark at every customer."

"Fine." José held up his hands in surrender. "Do whatever you want."

"You won't even know he's here." Mari smiled as she led Tabasco through the restaurant. He let out a bark and Mr. Ramirez immediately rolled his eyes.

"I already do," he mumbled. By now José Ramirez was so distraught by the last few days that he was finding it hard to breathe normally.

"Are you okay, dad?" Mari watched him long enough to convince herself that he would be fine.

"Only time will tell, Marisol. I can't believe I'm complaining about business, but we've been so overloaded with customers that I'm struggling to keep up. We need more help, but we can't afford to hire anyone yet. Besides, I have no idea how long this rush of customers is going to last. And don't even get me started on the way the police department has been watching my every move." He went into his office and sat down.

Mari kept the events of her frightening night to herself. He had enough on his plate and, according to Mari's mother, he had a hard time taming his temper. Mari could have found herself in the middle of an hour long lecture about minding her own business and never trusting her brothers' judgment.

Because the family was still struggling to accommodate the new wave of guests that were visiting the restaurant since the murder, Mari's mother and grandmother showed up to help during the lunch rush. Her mom welcomed customers while her Abuela stood in the back making tortillas and grilling vegetables.

Mari joined her Abuela in the kitchen and made guacamole according to her mother's recipe. It called for extra lime and cilantro. The lack of new meats rapidly pushed the family toward a crisis, but the crisis was at least two or three days away, and today Mari had resolved not to worry about it. There was simply too much else to worry about, what with her dad refusing to come out of his office and Mateo coming in early to help out with food prep.

In most circumstances, Mari would have welcomed Mateo's help but the memories of last night were still fresh in her mind. While she had no idea who had broken into Steve's office, Mateo was high on the list of suspects. He had left work early the previous night and was vague about where he was going. What had he been up to? Mari wanted to find out.

With the absence of an explanation, Mari's imagination ran wild. When her grandmother stepped out to use the restroom, leaving her alone with Mateo for a couple of minutes, she nearly panicked. It didn't help that Tabasco had escaped from the office and was following Mari around. Tabasco had never shown any hostility towards Mateo before, but today he emitted constant growling that occasionally broke into loud barks. Mari knew from experience that Tabasco only behaved this way when he smelled something fishy. Sometimes literally. It made Mari wonder why Tabasco had barked at Steve so much in the week before he died.

As soon as David and Alex arrived, Mari took them into a back room and explained what had happened the night before.

"How much do we know about Mateo?" Mari asked.

"Mari, he's not your killer," David commented. "Or your robber. Believe me; this isn't a road you want to go down."

"What makes you so sure? He's been working here for a few months and in that time I've learned absolutely zilch about him. He's the most evasive person ever. Mateo never answers my questions. He never has a good explanation for why he's leaving early."

"Take it from us," Alex responded, "people have their own lives. Mateo is just being a guy."

"But that doesn't cut it when there's a murder involved," Mari disagreed. "There's no room for privacy here. We need to find out everything we can about him."

"Mari, don't blow this out of proportion," David said.

"I'm not." Mari glared at him. "David, this mystery isn't going to solve itself."

"The police might," Alex said in a very quiet voice.

The three of them went on arguing about Mateo like until the end of their lunch break, and then the two boys returned to the dining room. As Mari headed toward the restroom, she saw that the back door was wide open once again. Her heart pounded. She hadn't seen anyone come in, or anyone go out.

CHAPTER TWELVE

The restaurant closed briefly in the afternoon to prepare for the dinner crowd. Mr. Ramirez usually remained in his office until about an hour before the restaurant opened again. He came out before the dinner rush and announced that Tabasco would be locked up for the duration of the evening and that anyone who put up an argument would be fired. Of course, he had said that before. Mr. Ramirez picked the dog up off the floor and carried him to the back room.

The crowd that night was smaller than the one the night before, but Mr. and Mrs. Ramirez were still exhausted when the restaurant closed an hour later than normal. Mari's mom went into the kitchen to make herself a light meal while her dad warmed up some rice and refried beans.

"You kids need to go home," Mrs. Ramirez said, taking a bite of a soft taco. "Take the rest of the night off. Your papa and I will handle this."

"That wouldn't be fair to you, though," Mari responded, who was determined to remain in her father's good graces. "I'm not leaving this restaurant until you do."

"Well, that's noble of you, but we can handle it on our own." Paula took a deep breath. "You need to rest up for the breakfast burrito crowd."

"Mari is right," Chrissy chimed in. "Sorry to interrupt Mrs. Ramirez but it wouldn't be fair to y'all for the rest of us to bail and leave you with the clean-up. I'll stay."

Chrissy, Mari, and Mari's parents all turned to look at David and Alex as if expecting them to make a similar declaration. The resigned look on their faces indicated that they would stay because they couldn't see any way out of it, but they weren't happy about it.

"I have to go, actually," Mateo said in a low voice. "I already made plans for tonight. Sorry. Eh, lo siento." He turned and walked out of the dining room before anyone had a chance to respond.

"Okay, what is his deal?" Mari asked out loud.

"I think he has a girlfriend in another town," David replied. "And probably a kid. That would explain the look of defeat in his eyes."

"David," his mother Paula scolded him. "Having children is a great blessing. It's when they get older that really takes its toll."

"With the exception of David and me," Alex added. "Right, mom?"

"I gave up on you two long ago," Paula answered jokingly. Alex shrugged in response.

"Fine. We will stay tonight and help you clean." David paused and studied the look of awe on his mother's face.

"We will?" Alex muttered to his brother. "Uh, don't we have that *thing*?"

"Thing?" David repeated curiously. His eyes widened. "Oh yes, the *thing*. How could I forget?"

"Homework?" their father guessed. "It better be homework. If I'm paying for night school, you sure as habaneros shouldn't be goofing around."

"Homework, yes," Alex said in response. But as Alex and David headed for the back door, Mari cornered them.

"Where are you *really* going?" Mari whispered, glancing over her shoulder where her coworkers were hard at work.

"To do some snooping," David answered. "It's all in the name of the restaurant."

"Translation, please." Mari clenched her jaw.

David nodded sagely. "We're going to follow Mateo so you can shut up about him once and for all. He's not a murderer, Mari. I put Alex's phone in the back of his car so I can track him using GPS."

"Hey." Alex felt his empty pockets. "Why does it always have to be my phone, bro?"

"We'll get it back." David chuckled.

"Just don't get caught," Mari responded, trying to hide the fact that she was actually impressed by the idea.

"We never do," David reminded her. He nudged Alex, and the two of them disappeared into the night.

Mari joined Chrissy wiping down tables. Chrissy returned to her favorite topic of conversation, which was the murder of Steve

Wilson. Chrissy liked to talk no matter the circumstance.

"I always got the sense that Steve was smitten with me," Chrissy said. "The thing I could never figure out was how many girls he felt that way about. I know he was very lonely, and maybe he would've hooked up with anyone. But I like to think *we* were special."

"We?" Mari repeated. She couldn't help but recite in her mind, *there is no we.* "Sure. Maybe. But it's sad to think that his brain limited himself to the women of this restaurant. It's too bad he didn't get out much. Out of this town, I mean."

"Oh, he did," Chrissy responded. "Steve always told stories to impress me, and he loved to talk about the year he went to China. Yep. That was a trip he seemed to love. Oh, well."

"China?" Mari said weakly, as a thought occurred to her.

Chrissy nodded, wringing her cloth over a bucket full of water. "His favorite story was the one where a giant black tortoise chased him on the Great Wall of China." She laughed. "It's silly, isn't it?"

"The picture," Mari stated, but Chrissy didn't seem to hear her. "That's where he was standing in that picture in his office." She quickly shut her mouth before Chrissy paid her any attention.

"Steve always talked about wanting to visit Russia someday, and now I wish he had gotten to go." Chrissy let out a sigh. "He used to speak to me in Chinese, just to show off. I think he might've traveled the world if he had had more money."

Mari excused herself to go to the bathroom. A whole new possibility had just opened up in her mind, and she couldn't believe she hadn't seen it before. Mari tried calling Alex, but he didn't answer. She only belatedly remembered that his phone was in the back of Mateo's car. Cursing herself for her forgetfulness and praying he had remembered to put the phone on silent, she called David instead. But David didn't answer either. His phone went straight to voicemail.

CHAPTER THIRTEEN

After Chrissy had left for the night, Mari continued to call David. Each time she failed to reach him, she waited a few minutes and then tried again. Mari wondered where her brothers were and whether or not they had found Mateo. She hoped David's lack of response was a sign that they were busy solving the mystery of where Mateo went every night.

The fact that Steve had spent a year in China following graduation shined a strange new light on the case. It was bizarre that she hadn't known this given how long Steve had been into her and how often they had talked. It was almost as if Steve hadn't wanted Mari to know. Mari asked herself why Steve would be embarrassed to talk about the most important trip of his life. Either he had been incredibly shy around her in a way he wasn't around Chrissy, or it was all lies to impress a pretty face.

No, Steve went to China. He had a picture to prove it. Mari felt a sort of quiet sadness when she realized that Steve's trip was around the time she had turned him down for prom. Had he gone to China to get away from her? Of course, Steve would have never talked about it in front of her because it had been an embarrassing subject.

"Maybe I was all wrong about Steve?" Mari said to Tabasco, who looked up at her with big curious eyes. "Maybe I should have given him a chance?" She exhaled loudly. "Or maybe I'm talking crazy because it's so late?"

Mari shook her head, trying to get rid of the regrets that haunted her. How had she never known Steve had spoken a second language? And now, as it happened, that little fact could end up being the key to the whole mystery.

Mari tried calling David again. When the phone went to voicemail, she left a message.

"David, it's me," Mari said. "Listen. I just found out that Steve spent a year in *China*, and could speak the language too. Crazy, right? I think the murderer might be Mr. Chun. I think he might have killed him because…I don't know. Anyway, call me back as soon as you get this."

Mari wasn't sure the last part of her message had been clear because Tabasco had started barking about halfway through. He was watching the back door and baring his teeth. This was unusual behavior from him. Tabasco didn't bark unless there was something or someone to bark at.

Mari gulped, her heart pounding. Once again she was alone in an empty building, and unarmed. She had been in this situation too many times in the last couple of days for her liking.

Mari was tempted to make a run for the car, but curiosity, and a certain stubbornness compelled her. Was there really someone outside or did Tabasco see things? Mari didn't know. Moving as quietly as she could into the kitchen, she crouched low behind a counter and waited. If it were nothing, she would have peace of mind. But if it *were* someone, her nosiness would have put her in harm's way yet again.

A flashlight shot out of the darkness. Footsteps sounded on the gravel in the back parking lot and echoed all the way into the kitchen. The footsteps came closer and closer, eventually entering the restaurant. Mari wasn't alone anymore. Mari slowly reached up and opened a drawer, drawing out a long knife.

Wild thoughts darted through Mari's mind as she sat there cradling the knife in one hand. Maybe it was a staff member? Mari rubbed her forehead and reminded herself that none of them would have broken in through the back entrance.

If it were Chrissy coming to collect something she had forgotten, she would have knocked or called her first.

Rising slowly from her hiding place, Mari called for Tabasco. As soon as the dog came to her, Mari panicked and shut the kitchen doors. She immediately locked them as she thought of barricading herself inside for the night. Not even a hot plate of Carne Asada could save her now.

CHAPTER FOURTEEN

BOOM!

Someone pounded on the kitchen door.

BOOM!

The culprit tried kicking the door open. Whoever it was possessed a savage energy, and there was no telling what the intruder might do next. Mari cringed at each bang that rang through her ears.

With one shaky hand, Mari called the police. With the other, she tried to silence Tabasco whose barking threatened to drown out her words completely.

"Yes, this is Mari Ramirez," Mari shouted into the phone. "I'm at Lito Bueno's Mexican Restaurant and someone just broke into the restaurant. I'm alone. Please, hurry!"

The dispatcher said police were on their way. Mari hung up and texted her parents.

The pounding continued. Whoever was out there was determined to get to Mari. She prayed that the intruder wouldn't attempt to get in through one of the kitchen windows. She had accidentally broken one playing softball with some friends when she was seven, and it hadn't been difficult.

BOOM!

The noise was like a battering ram breaking down the walls of a medieval castle. Plates shook. Paintings swung precariously on the walls where they hung.

Mari regretted not running for her dad's office instead of the kitchen. The office had a lock and no windows. Mari might have had a better chance at keeping the intruder away from her in that room. Of course, they weren't any kitchen knives in the office.

Tabasco continued with his barking until the pounding outside of the door suddenly stopped. For a moment, the air was deadly still. And then Mari heard the sound of shoes on gravel.

Mari gasped as light illuminated a kitchen window in front of her. Instinctively she closed her eyes, as though preparing for a loud noise and shattered glass.

The flashlight moved on, leaving darkness behind it, and the footsteps receded into the distance.

Sirens were approaching.

Mari was safe. For now.

***

Mari made a pot of tea for herself and Detective Price. She held the mug in her hands, drinking slowly, struggling to calm herself down.

"I think I know who it was," Mari said shakily. "I think I know who broke in. And possibly who murdered Steve."

"Who do you think it was?" Detective Price asked with evident skepticism.

Mari took a deep breath before saying, "It was Mr. Chun." Her voice sounded panicky, and her words came out rushed. "I know because Steve once went to China, and he could speak fluent Chinese. Something was going on between them although I don't know what."

She felt herself slowly deflating. The words had sounded so much more convincing in her own head. Now Mari felt like an idiot. The blood ran into her face.

"I will keep that in mind," Detective Price responded as he placed his ever-present notepad back in his shirt pocket. "In the meantime, I suggest you go home and get some rest."

"But aren't you even going to look into it?" Mari asked, upset that he had seemed to brush aside her theory.

"Look, I'll be honest with you." Detective Price glanced in her direction. "I have no idea if Mr. Chun tried to break in tonight, but I can assure you he didn't murder Steve Wilson. He was at home that entire morning. His wife has vouched for him. Mr. Chun has a solid alibi."

Mari wanted to protest. Of course, Mr. Chun's wife would vouch for her husband. They were obviously in cahoots with each other. But Mari kept her mouth shut, knowing that there wasn't much else she could say. She had no solid evidence.

There was a knock on the door of the office, and Detective Price stood to open it. It was Mrs. Ramirez. The moment Paula saw her daughter, she hugged her tight.

"You have no idea how worried I was," Paula said. "You have no idea how worried your father is. He wanted to come down here himself, but I told him I would handle it. I haven't seen him so distressed in ages. He wasn't even this scared when he thought he might lose his business."

Mari planted herself deeper into her mother's embrace.

"Do you want some hot chocolate?" said Mrs. Ramirez asked her daughter. "I'll make you Abuela's specialty."

Mari knew that hot chocolate was her mother's way of showing love, and she couldn't refuse.

"We'll have a drink," Paula said. "Then I'll take you home."

CHAPTER FIFTEEN

Mari was feeling rattled by the time her mother escorted her home. In the last couple of days, an intruder had broken into Steve's office while she was searching it, and someone had tried to break into the restaurant. Mari was beginning to wonder if maybe she was cursed.

"Stay with me, please," Mari said to her mom as they stood in the living room together.

"I have to get home to your father," said Mrs. Ramirez replied. "Just keep the door locked and let Tabasco stand guard for the night."

"Okay." Mari sighed.

When her mother had left, Mari didn't even bother changing into her pajamas. She stared at herself in the mirror for what felt like hours as she brushed her teeth. She double checked her front door a few times before crashing into her bed.

Mari couldn't help feeling that the police were being singularly unhelpful. Detective Price had stood there pretending to listen as she'd presented what she had discovered about Steve and how it could have been related to Mr. Chun. But the detective was still hung up on Mari's father. The scales of justice in this town were weighted against her dad and his restaurant.

Up until now the hardest moment of Mari's life had been coming home after breaking off her engagement and trying to start over. But even in doing that there had been a measure of peace. She had been welcomed by her family. Her life hadn't been in danger, and no one had been trying to kill her. Steve's death had ended all that.

Mari figured that Steve's ghost was somewhere now smiling at her misfortune.

Tabasco leaped up on the bed, his fawn and white face pointed at the bedroom door. He bared his teeth in a menacing fashion. When Mari put down a hand to silence him, she felt the tension in his body.

"Tabasco, hush," she pleaded, but he barked louder and louder.

And then she heard a banging on her front door.

Mari got out of bed, her boldness increasing with each step she took. Unlocking the door of her bedroom and flipping on the light, she glared at her front door.

"I suppose the time has come, Tabasco," she whispered, her voice quivering. "This is what I get for trying to help."

A chill ran down Mari's spine as she looked through her peephole and saw nothing. Her front porch was empty. A cool breeze rushed across her arms, and Mari noticed that a window had been opened. She jumped as a laugh came from shadows. A figure stepped into the light. It was Desh, Mr. Chun's nephew.

"Three break-ins in two days," Mari said as calmly as she could, realizing too late that she had no weapon to defend herself. "And finally we meet face-to-face. Again."

"I thought I would drop by," Desh responded.

It was the first time she had heard him speak English. He wasn't bad at it.

"You speak pretty good English for someone who only speaks Chinese," Mari commented. "But I know practicing your English isn't the real reason you're here."

"You're right about that," Desh said with a smirk on his face. He glared at Tabasco as he continued to bark. "I have other items of business to tend to tonight." He held up a slender object.

Mari's heart jolted into her throat as she realized it was a knife.

"So you did kill Steve Wilson," Mari said, trying to appear calm while she thought of a plan.

"Yes," Desh proudly replied. "My you have many questions."

"I don't get it," Mari continued, eyeing her kitchen sink. "Why Steve? Did you even know him?"

"Not really," he replied. "But the idiot got in my way and even tried blackmailing me."

Mari stared at him, puzzled.

"What for?"

Tabasco kept himself in between Desh and Mari as Desh slowly inched forward.

"That's my business," Desh said. "I couldn't let my uncle find out what I've been doing at his restaurant, or he would put a stop to it. That's why

Steve had to go. He wanted my money and my dignity."

"He did need the money." Mari clenched her fists tight.

Suddenly, Tabasco lunged forward, biting Desh's leg. He howled in pain. Seizing her opportunity, Mari ran through the living room, pushing past him. He made a weak attempt to grab her, but she brushed him aside and kept running.

Mari slammed the door behind her to buy herself a few seconds. She then ran down the stairs two at a time and bounded off into the dark streets.

CHAPTER SIXTEEN

Mari sprinted down the street. She heard the sound of footsteps rattling down the concrete stairs that led to her apartment stairs behind her.

As long as she stayed on the main road and in the glow of the street lamps, Mari knew she had a better chance of surviving. Desh was quick, and already he seemed to be gaining on her. Her best chance was to alert the neighborhood to the fact that she was being attacked.

"HELP! HELP!" Mari shouted, panic overpowering the sense of embarrassment she felt. "PLEASE, HELP!"

Lights began flickering on throughout the apartment complex. Doors opened, and random strangers poked their heads into the night to see what was going on.

"CALL THE POLICE!" Mari yelled with her last ounce of breath.

There was no use continuing to run. Mari was already winded, and Desh was just a few yards behind. She would have to use her smarts to outwit him and keep herself alive until help came.

Mari let out a yell and swung around just as Desh caught up to her. She punched him in the face and sent him staggering backward. Desh grabbed his nose with one hand, looking disappointed that Mari had temporarily disarmed him. The punch seemed to have surprised Desh more than anything.

At that moment, a blue Honda Civic pulled up beside Mari. Its tires screeched, and Mari smiled. To her immense relief, the doors flew open, and David and Alex leaped out.

"I think we've had about enough of you," David said, grabbing Desh by the collar.

"You'll have to tell us what the food's like in prison," Alex added, kneeing him firmly in the stomach for good measure. Desh winced in pain and doubled over. "On second thought, I don't want to know unless they've got chimichangas."

The back door on the passenger's side of the car opened, and Mateo stepped out. He looked remarkably alert as if the prospect of catching a murderer had suddenly woken him from the lethargy in which he normally operated. "Are you going to tell her or should I?" Mateo looked from David to Alex.

"Fine," Alex responded, placing one arm around Mateo. "We suspected someone was dealing drugs out of the Lucky Noodle, so we got Mateo to help us out. He posed as a high-schooler looking to score some dope, and it worked. Desh here hasn't been around long enough to know that he works for us."

"And he's stupid," David added to Alex's explanation.

"Anything to help a friend," Mateo chimed in. "Wouldn't want the police pinning it on your family's restaurant. Creeps like Desh do that sort of thing all the time."

"Which must have been what Steve knew." Mari sighed. "That was the information that got him killed." To her great surprise, Desh spoke up.

"He was threatening to expose the entire operation," Desh shouted in a venomous voice. "He kept taunting me, in Chinese, about the money he was going to squeeze out of me. I made the mistake of talking about what I was up to while he was nearby. How was I supposed to know that he spoke Chinese?'"

"He needed the money," said Mari explained. "He would have done anything to keep his business from going under. I guess that's exactly what he did. Steve heard Desh talking about his illegal side business, and Steve saw it as his opportunity to make some dough."

By now a crowd had gathered around them. People came in their robes and slippers to gawk at the scene in front of them. David had his arms wrapped tightly around Desh as though he were giving him a hug. Mari explained the story again for the benefit of her new audience as Alex called the police.

"They're almost here," Alex said, hanging up the phone. "Apparently they've already received calls from about a dozen people."

Mateo came toward Mari and inhaled sharply, looking a bit bashful. "I just wanted to say that I'm sorry for being weird lately. I've actually enrolled in night school for the last couple of months. I didn't want to tell y'all because I didn't want to jeopardize my job."

"But why have you been coming in early when you didn't have to?" Mari asked.

"To make up for all the lost time," Mateo said, turning crimson. "Plus, I was kind of hoping you'd notice."

CHAPTER SEVENTEEN

One week later, Mari's family and fellow staff members threw an enormous party at Lito Bueno's Mexican Restaurant. Four tables had been pushed together in the center of the room, and on them was spread a festive red and white tablecloth. The tables were filled with silver trays of roasted shrimp, homemade flour and corn tortillas, shredded pork, chimichangas, green peppers stuffed with cheese and cilantro, grilled corn, and lime steak tortas. Mari piled her plate high with guacamole, chips, and roasted salsa.

At the center of each table in the dining room stood a vase with a colorful flower arrangement. Paper flowers on strings hung from the rafters and bright serapes of red, green, and purple covered each wall. Cactus candlesticks and lemonade pitchers lined the bar. Even Mari's dad had gotten into the spirit of the occasion, wearing a striped green scarf, while Mari had dressed Tabasco in a multicolored poncho.

"I don't like that dog, Mari," Mari's Abuela said in Spanish as the dining hall began to swell with people.

"He's really not that bad," Mari replied. "He's a sweetheart once you get to know him."

"Yes, but he *slobbers*." She made a face of disgust. "I can't stand it when dogs slobber."

"Babies slobber all over the place," Alex chimed in.

"Babies are cute," Mari's Abuela stated in Spanish.

Mari laughed.

"Honestly it's a wonder he hasn't run away," her Abuela went on, "the way the back door keeps being left open."

Mari fixed her with a shrewd look. "Have *you* been leaving the back door open, Abuela?"

Her Abuela just laughed and walked away.

"Grandmothers," Alex commented, taking a huge bite of a bean burrito smothered in queso. The queso dripped down his chin. "Cheers, family. Desh has been taken into custody, we found a new meat delivery man, and Dad is a free bird."

"Plus, business is booming," Mari reminded the group. "We might have to open another restaurant just to seat everyone."

Mateo came over and placed his hand snugly in Mari's. "I'll drink to that."

"I'd like to propose a toast," José Ramirez said, lightly tapping his glass. "To Lito Bueno's, the best Mexican restaurant in town."

The only Mexican restaurant in town, Mari thought. But she proudly joined in as all her family and friends raised their glasses and said with one voice, "The *best* Mexican restaurant in town."

A Preview of **UNTIL DEATH DO US TART** by Holly Plum

CHAPTER ONE

Five minutes from the sugar sands of the Florida coast was a sweet little town, and it was just a slow walk down humid Main Street to the pink lacquered doors of Patty Cakes Bake Shop. Inside was a blast of air conditioning and an irresistible display of sweets of all kinds. Some were a little lopsided, but others were so perfect it was as though they had been lifted out of a baking magazine and popped right into the case.

In the back of the shop was a modest kitchen where Joy Cooke was whisking egg whites and sugar by hand. She had a smear of cocoa on her cheek, flour dusted her apron, and flecks of confectioner's sugar made her dark hair look prematurely gray for a woman in her mid-thirties. A stand mixer sat motionless on the bench. Joy paused to crack another egg white into the bowl and stretched her wrist before resuming her ferocious whisking with all of her might. She was determined to beat the whites into a stiff meringue, or to at least work some of her stress out trying.

Joy had woken very early that day with a feeling that something was *coming*. It wasn't quite dread, but it was close. She couldn't shake it — she'd felt all day as though something was brewing, hovering over her; as though she had left sweet buns to rise somewhere and they were all going to fall flat if she didn't tend to them soon. But there was nothing she was meant to do. She had spent the day checking and double-checking everything she did, opening and closing every drawer, double counting the change she gave customers, and keeping track of everything she sold. She shook her head and sighed, quickening her whisking to an unbelievable speed. She had no idea what could be giving her such anxiety.

Sara Beth, Joy's assistant, stood in the doorway with a hand on her hip and the other holding a jumbo cup of iced tea. She was a Southern belle who had swanned into the bakery six months before and talked her way into a job. Though Sara Beth was charming enough that she could convince anyone to do anything, Joy had no regrets about having hired her. Sara Beth was the best assistant Joy could have hoped for. She was talkative, creative, and most of all – loyal.

"You know, ma'am," Sara Beth took a sip of her tea and let the straw pop off her lips in a way that always meant *I'm about to tell it like it is,* "I believe there is a faster way to make meringue. One that won't give you arthritis." Sara Beth took another sip and motioned with her head towards the neglected mixer in the corner.

Joy looked up and smiled, shaking her head. "You know what I always say, Sara Beth. Mama's recipes are –"

"Recipes for success," they said in unison. Sara Beth rolled her eyes but laughed, which always made Joy smile. In the time she'd known her assistant, Sara Beth had brought a bright light into the bakery that was much needed.

Joy's mother, Patty, had started a home bakery when Joy was young. Joy's earliest memories were of helping squeeze oranges for her mother's signature yellow Florida cake with cream cheese and marmalade frosting. By the time Joy was ten years old, her mom had sold enough cakes, tarts and cookies to set up her own bake shop downtown. "The real deal," Patty had called it as they'd stood together on the street, holding hands and watching the sign writer put the finishing touches on the cursive *Patty Cakes Bake Shop* sign.

The shop had become a raging success as soon as it had opened. Patty had joked that it was always hot in the kitchen because the door swung open every five seconds. Since Patty had unexpectedly passed away two years ago, the regulars had stayed loyal to the bakery even though Joy Cooke often had a hard time living up to her mother's name. Joy followed Patty's foolproof recipes down to the letter. Including a handwritten note her mother had jotted down when the bake shop had first opened. The note said to hand mix everything.

Joy sighed as she beat the eggs, wondering if she'd ever really live up to either part of her name – the *Joy* or the *Cooke*. Joy's bemoaning was cut short by the chime of the bell above the front door. She and Sara Beth looked at each other.

Sara Beth cocked her head to the side. "Could she really be *that* early?"

She could.

Crystal Stone pushed open the pink doors of Patty Cakes Bake Shop with all her might and felt immediately relieved by the energy in the room. Or maybe it was the cool blast of air conditioning. Crystal was a firm believer in karma, and reading messages from the universe. Whether it was cool vibes or cool air conditioning, Crystal was sure she was in the right place. Her necklaces and bracelets jingled as she walked into the shop. Sara Beth popped out from the kitchen.

"I'm early," Crystal announced. "I know I'm such a pain, but I was meditating this morning like I always do and I have a very strong feeling that I need to re-try these cakes *immediately*. That's why I'm early."

Sara Beth stood smiling for a moment to process Crystal's request.

"Of course, ma'am. Come on in. We've set up a table for you." Luckily, Sara Beth had not left her southern hospitality in Mississippi when she'd moved to Florida.

She led Crystal to the bay window and the largest table in the shop, which Joy had decorated with white linen and lilies in preparation for the cake tasting.

"Would you like to wait for your fiancé here while we get the new samples ready?" Sara Beth asked.

Crystal inhaled as she sat, and put a hand to her heart. "No, Lucas won't be joining me."

"Oh, my. Is everything alright?"

Crystal reached out and touched Sara Beth's hand. Her engagement ring had spun around on her finger, and the gigantic amethyst stone dug into Sara Beth's palm. "We're right as rain, darling. He's working late and couldn't make it today. I'm always early, and he's always late. That's how it seems to go with us. I'm up at dawn to teach yoga, and he's out at night with clients."

"So sorry to hear that." Sara Beth tutted sympathetically and carefully pulled her hand back. She lay a cloth napkin on Crystal's lap.

"Stress is a manageable thing, Sara Beth," Crystal inhaled and exhaled loudly, "You just have to breathe through it. Breathe with me, Sara Beth."

Joy had raced to the bathroom to make herself look more presentable, leaving her egg whites to deflate into a gloopy mess. She joined Sara Beth looking a little rough around the edges with her tightly curled hair never behaving quite the way she wished it would.

"Hi there, Crystal," Joy greeted her client. "It's good to see you again."

It wasn't a pleasure. This was the fourth time Crystal had changed her mind about the cake she wanted for her wedding, and her wedding date was right around the corner. Joy needed Crystal to decide on a flavor today and stick to it if she was going to prepare the cake in time.

"Joy, what a *joy* you are." Crystal stood to kiss Joy on each cheek.

"Is Lucas on his way?" Joy asked.

"No, but it's probably better that way. He's so stressed about the wedding that he's oozing with negative vibes at the moment. We don't want those around my wedding cake." Crystal took a deep breath.

All Joy knew about Crystal's fiancé Lucas was that he'd liked the last four cakes just fine. She smiled politely as Sara Beth presented the samples for Crystal to taste.

The first cake sample was a red velvet cake. The flavor that Crystal had decided was the one she wanted last week. Normally, the red color of the cake appeared when traditional cocoa, vinegar, and buttermilk reacted. But Crystal's dietary requirements meant that no dairy could be used in the cake, leaving Joy to create the red color by using beet puree. Joy was particularly proud of her substitution, having licked the bowl clean herself.

"It's just ... my intuition says this isn't perfect," Crystal sighed, placing her fork down after a small bite.

"Alright, on to the next." Sara Beth quickly passed Crystal a slice of lemon poppy seed cake. It was spongy, light, and delicate. Crystal took a bite and closed her eyes as the cake melted in her mouth. It was the perfect of amount of tartness mixed with the perfect amount of sweetness. But it was too spongey for Crystal's taste.

Next, there was a vanilla cake with salted caramel. The saltiness balanced perfectly with the sweet, sticky caramel, but Crystal insisted the salt was *too beachy*. Since the wedding was at an elegant beachside manor, she didn't want her guests thinking they were eating sand. Joy tried not to take offense.

The macadamia and coconut cake was almost a hit before Crystal remembered that Lucas was allergic to macadamia nuts.

It was during the tasting of the orange pistachio cake that Crystal looked up at the framed photograph of Joy's mom above the cash register. She stopped chewing and swallowed deeply, her eyes on the portrait.

"This woman." Crystal let out a long sigh as if it were her personal duty to deliver some kind of message from the other side. "She has passed on, am I right?"

Joy nodded, her hand placed on her heart. She'd seen psychics on television but had never visited one before. Joy preferred to keep her head out of the clouds. But her pulse raced at the idea that her mom might be trying to send her a message. Maybe that's why she had been feeling different all day.

"I'm in the process of developing my psychic gifts," Crystal continued. "Let me see." Before Joy had a chance to reply, Crystal held up her hand and began. "The woman in the photo was your ... um ... I'm getting something."

Crystal closed her eyes, hummed in a high-pitched tune, and made a face like she'd just eaten a lemon tart that was a little too sour.

Sara Beth cleared her throat.

"She's your ... Oh! Oh, I see it. She's your long lost aunt twice removed?" Crystal opened one eye and looked at Joy.

"That's my mother," Joy answered. "Her name was Patty. She opened this shop. But thank you for trying."

"Hmm." Crystal slouched in her chair and pouted at the portrait. "That's odd. You would think she'd at least want to talk to me about the cakes I'm trying."

"I'm not sure I understand." Joy did her best to smile politely.

"My mother has passed on too," Crystal went on. "Though she never left me anything quite as magnificent as this shop. Just left me with Dad, who also passed away, leaving me with a step mother who is a real shrew. Pardon my language, but my step-mother would love it if I ordered this awful orange pistachio cake for the wedding. No offense."

"Try the chocolate, ma'am." Sara Beth shoved the next plate under Crystal's nose before she could say anything else.

"Well, look at that." Crystal's full attention was suddenly on the cake. "Beautiful. Simply beautiful." And beautiful it was. A slice of Joy's specialty – double dark chocolate. The cake was so dark that light couldn't escape from it. Crystal easily sunk her fork into the sample, the moist frosting melting in her mouth.

"Thank the cosmos," Crystal exclaimed. The sweetness of the frosting touched her tongue first, followed by the slightest hint of bitterness from the dark chocolate, rounded out by a pinch of Joy's secret spice blend – cinnamon, cardamom, vanilla and a pinch from the jar in the kitchen labeled *Patty's Secret Spice*. Even Joy had no idea what was in there, but it was included in every chocolate recipe and brought the flavors together like magic.

"I'm glad you like it," Joy commented.

"This is the one," Crystal mumbled through a mouthful. "It's perfect." She tapped her feet excitedly as she ate the entire piece.

"So we have a winner?" Sara Beth asked, hopefully.

"Have you made your decision?" Joy asked, skeptically.

"I certainly have," Crystal answered. "I want chocolate. *All* chocolate. But I simply can't wait to taste that chocolate again until I'm married. Do you have a piece I can take home for my darling Lucas? He's going to die when he tastes this."

"Sorry," Sara Beth chimed in. "The chocolate cake is our best seller. We're out at the moment."

Crystal huffed, disappointed. "I suppose I could pick up something chocolatey on my way home. What's the name of that other bakery across town? The Sugar Room?"

Joy took a sharp inhale at the mention of her dastardly competition, ready to launch into a tirade about underhanded marketing tactics and unethical baking tricks.

"But our chocolate tart is truly to die for." Sara Beth pushed past Joy and presented a tart to Crystal. "It's the same chocolate taste as the cake, and it's dairy-free. We made lots of our dairy-free desserts today because we knew you were coming. The Sugar Room doesn't make anything dairy-free."

The tart shined with perfectly tempered chocolate, the serene surface only broken where it was studded with delicate chocolate bark. The crust was golden brown, and Crystal swallowed in anticipation of cutting into it.

"Yum." Crystal sighed in adoration. Her eyes glazed over as though she were suddenly hypnotized. "It's so *dark*. One bite and you could just melt into nothingness."

Sara Beth caught Joy's eye behind Crystal's back and circled her finger around her ear, insinuating that Crystal was a little crazy. Joy couldn't help smirking. The closer she got to her wedding day, the more Crystal's mood could be turned on and off like a light switch.

Suddenly the clanging of Crystal's jewelry echoed through the shop as she clapped her hands together and bounced joyously in her seat. "Lucas will love it. I'll take it!"

"Fantastic." Sara Beth joined in the rejoicing. "A sweetie for your sweetie."

"A little taste of our wedding for my groom to be," Crystal said. "I love that idea."

Sara Beth boxed up the tart while Joy took Crystal's down payment for the wedding cake. Still rattled by the mention of The Sugar Room, and happy to have finally secured a deposit, Joy gave Crystal the tart for free.

Joy and Sara Beth stood shoulder to shoulder and bid farewell to the bride-to-be, watching Crystal load the tart into her bicycle basket.

Joy mumbled, "Is the tart going to survive?"

"Is the marriage going survive?" Sara Beth snorted.

* * *

Sara Beth was closing up the bake shop and stacking the chairs as the sunset painted the coastal town cupcake pink. Joy was recounting the perfectly balanced cash register for the fourth time when the bell above the front door chimed.

"Hello," a well-dressed man entered, dabbing sweat from his brow with a handkerchief.

"Hi there, sir. We're closing for the day, but I can pack you up something to-go." Joy eyed the limited selection of baked goods.

The man walked slowly to the counter, looking around the whole shop. He paused before spotting the glass case and moved over to inspect it.

"This is your selection?" he asked.

"Yes, sir." Joy frowned, unsure what to make of him. She was used to the pleasant conversation from most of her customers.

"What's this?" the man motioned to something behind the glass.

Sara Beth looked over his shoulder and replied cheerfully, "That's a mini pineapple cheesecake. It's one of my favorites."

"Oh?" The man looked at Sara Beth's winning smile and softened a little. "Do you have any chocolate tarts leftover?"

"I'm afraid we sold the last one today. But the chocolate babka is-" Sara Beth was cut off.

"Did you sell a chocolate tart to a ...," the man fished a hand into his pocket and retrieved his notepad. "... a Mr. Tony Florentine?"

"Not that I recall," Joy answered. "All the tarts we sold to today were to locals. People I know personally. I don't know anyone named *Tony*."

"Are you the owner of this establishment miss ..."

"Joy Cooke." Joy's heart began to race. "And yes, I own this shop. What can I do for you?" Joy balled her hands into lose fists, waiting for a bout of bad news. Surely this man was a health inspector who had been given a false tip by The Sugar Room. Joy was certain the owner, Maple McWayne, would stop at nothing to put her out of business.

"I'm Detective Sugar, and I need to ask you a few questions." The man looked around again. "May I take a look at your kitchen?"

The detective helped himself. He opened and shut drawers and cabinets, and he even sniffed multiple bags of flour. He asked questions about the bake shop's cleaning routines, chemicals kept on the property, and who else had access to the kitchen. Joy answered his questions shakily but truthfully, while Sara Beth stood in the doorway nervously sipping sweet tea. Detective Sugar's gaze landed on the large ceramic canister of *Patty's Secret Spice*.

"What's this?" he picked up the canister and immediately shook it.

Joy grabbed it from him and held it close to her chest. She had had just about enough. "What is this about, detective?"

"Ma'am," he sighed, getting out his handkerchief and wiping his hands clean. "I'm sorry for my intrusion, but this is rather a difficult situation. I'm investigating a possible homicide. A man has died after eating a single slice of a chocolate tart from this establishment."

Sara Beth gasped, "Crystal? Please, don't say it was a woman named Crystal Stone."

"No," the detective responded. " I said a *man* has died."

Sara Beth gasped, "Lucas? Please don't say it was a man named Lucas."

"It was a man named Tony Florentine," he replied. "Are you certain neither of you know him?"

"I'm sorry, but I don't," Joy replied, still holding her mother's blend of spices close to her heart. "I can check the books, but I don't think it would help you much."

Joy looked to Sara Beth, who shook her head and shrugged.

"I'd appreciate any records you have, Joy." Detective Sugar crossed his arms. "I'm not saying you're a prime suspect, but I'm afraid your chocolate tart is guilty. I'll need samples of every ingredient in the shop, and I'll need to take this." He reached his hand out for Patty's secret blend of spices. "Don't worry. You'll get it back."

"I guess our chocolate tart really is to die for," Sara Beth muttered.

CHAPTER TWO

In the wake of the shocking visit by Detective Sugar, Joy and Sara Beth stood in the shop and watched him leave through the front windows. Joy was completely stunned. She could have stared out at the window all night, but Sara Beth broke her meditation as she scampered around the shop finishing her closing duties and gathering her belongings.

"Anyway, who on earth is Tony Florentine?" Sara Beth emptied out the last quart from a gallon of sweet tea into her cup.

Joy couldn't tell if Sara Beth's hands were shaky from nerves, or because that gallon of iced tea had been full in the morning, and Sara Beth was the only one to touch it.

"I've never heard the name," Joy answered. "But I suppose I don't know *everyone* in town even though my mind is a *trap* for names. You said so yourself." Joy tapped on her temple twice before glancing at her watch. "Head on out, Sara Beth. I'll finish up."

Sara Beth looked to Joy with a slight frown. "Are you sure? You look a little pale."

"Me?" Joy pinched her cheeks. "I'm fine. Really, I'm fine. I'll see you tomorrow."

Sara Beth was almost to the door when she turned back to smile to Joy. "Everything will be okay, Joy. Good things come to good people."

As Joy finished closing up the shop, she tried not to think about the chocolate tart and alleged manslaughter that could be on her hands. She also tried not to think about the possible rumors circulating around town, or the headline that could be splattered across the front of the newspaper tomorrow. The fact of the matter was that a man was dead. The victim could have been someone that Joy knew. With a different turn of fate, she could have killed someone else – a friend. Sara Beth's words echoed in her mind. *Everything will be okay.*

She shook her head as if to dismiss the thought, and went about packing up for the night.

Joy stepped out the back of the bakery and into the side street. The humidity felt like a warm blanket wrapped around her shoulders. Joy inhaled the seaside air. It was the best kind of medicine. She considered driving home by the beach that night – she'd left her fishing poles in the back of her car and casting her rod out into the waves was the best stress relief she'd ever found. And her cat, Cheesecake, would surely love a fresh fish treat.

Joy opened the trunk of her car to check on her equipment. An engine revved suddenly. She turned to look down the small, dark street and saw headlights driving towards her. The car sped up. Joy gasped, stunned by the blinding lights. The car came closer, acting as if it were about to slam into Joy. Joy felt as though she was stuck in quicksand. She couldn't move a muscle, or even breathe.

The car swerved away, just missing Joy. Joy let out a sigh of relief and turned just in time to see the street light illuminating the side of the car, and the logo stuck to the door – the frosted cupcake illustration of *The Sugar Room*.

* * *

Joy didn't stop at the beach. She drove straight home, though it took her twice as long as it normally did. She drove slowly and carefully. She was so shaken up that she couldn't stop tapping her finger on the steering wheel or thinking about her near-death experience.

How dare she? Joy asked herself. She was thinking about Maple McWayne, the owner, and manager of The Sugar Room. Maple certainly did not live up to her name, being the least sweet or delicate flavor of person that Joy had ever encountered. She had opened The Sugar Room after Patty Cakes Bake Shop had become popular, and had been using underhanded tactics to steal customers ever since.

The latest swindle happened after Joy was featured in an article in the local newspaper highlighting the shop's various selections of buttercream. The next week, Maple held a contest at the local senior center where The Sugar Room served free cupcakes and asked the residents to raise their hands if they agreed that the frosting was the best in town. Neither Joy nor any other baker in town was invited to compete. Now, a huge banner hung above The Sugar Room, proclaiming that it served the #1 best frosting in town.

Joy cursed at Maple. She wondered if Maple would really go so far as murder to shut down her business. Could she be desperate enough to kill somebody? Maybe the victim, Tony Florentine, wasn't supposed to die? Maybe Maple only intended to make Joy's customers ill, not kill them?

Joy shook the thought out of her head and reached into her glove compartment for a treat to calm her nerves. Popping a ginger chew in her mouth, she let the taste of the heat, spice and sweetness take her mind off Maple for a moment.

Joy's home was a beachside bungalow set amongst an overgrown tropical garden with a ceramic birdbath set on a small patch of grass. Fishing rods lined up beside the front door, and Joy entered her living room to find her cat Cheesecake sitting patiently on the sofa.

"You'll never guess what happened today, Cheesecake." Joy felt the day's weight start to lift off her chest as the chalk white cat jumped down and trotted over to her.

Cheesecake purred, weaving his way around her legs. Joy leaned down and scratched his cheeks.

"What a day I've had, my friend. What've you been doing all day, huh?" Joy sighed and plopped down onto the sofa, and grabbed the remote. Cheesecake jumped up into her lap, both of them lit by the television. "Sorry, no fresh fish for dinner. It'll have to be the usual tonight."

Joy channel surfed until she found an episode of *Make It Or Bake It*. It was one of her favorite cooking shows. Cheesecake immediately got up and left the room.

"Hey, I thought you liked this show?" Joy called after him.

Cheesecake scratched around in his litter box a little too loudly.

After a not-so-satisfying dinner of leftover casserole, Joy tossed and turned in bed. Cheesecake came and purred beside her, trying to soothe Joy to sleep.

"It's no good, Cheesecake," Joy whispered to him in the dark. "I'm worried about the bake shop."

Joy sighed and rolled onto her back, staring up at the ceiling.

"A man *died* because of a tart I made," Joy admitted. Cheesecake's purring stopped. Joy turned to look at him.

"It wasn't my fault. I didn't poison that chocolate tart. Of course, I didn't. Someone else did. Detective Sugar didn't give me any details." Joy cleared her throat. "I don't know. Maybe the man who died was just allergic to one of the ingredients."

Cheesecake began purring again.

"You're right," Joy continued. "Everything will be fine just like Sara Beth said."

Joy pulled the covers up to her chin. "Goodnight, Cheesecake. I love you, you little fuzz ball."

Joy finally got to sleep only to be woken in the middle of the night. She flicked her eyes open and sat up. She didn't know why she was awake at first, but suddenly she heard sounds coming from the kitchen. All the lights were out in the bungalow. It was almost pitch black except for a stream of moonlight barely illuminating her bedroom. The sounds stopped.

Joy strained her ears to hear anything else.

"Who's there?" she tried to make her voice sound deep and tough, but it came out as a croak.

CLANG.

Joy sat upright and held her breath. More unusual noises followed, and then the creak of the back door opening. Joy threw back the covers and ran down the hallway.

Her back porch was dark and still. The air was still humid with a cool, beach breeze, and the sound of ocean waves rang through the night. Joy grabbed a flashlight from under the kitchen sink and lit up her back porch. Nothing moved.

"Who's there?" Joy yelled out into the night.

The only reply was a squawking bird, Joy's racing heartbeat, and the echo of waves hitting the nearby shore.

CHAPTER THREE

The next day, Joy was sluggish and tired. As per usual, Cheesecake came into the bed to wake Joy as the sun came up. Joy was already wide awake after suffering a horrible nightmare that she was being drowned in a vat of molten chocolate.

"Oh, Cheesecake." Joy stroked her cat's fur coat. "Please, tell me that yesterday never happened." Cheesecake hardly blinked.

Joy dragged herself to the bake shop, reminding herself that starting the day off on a positive note was key to having a better day than yesterday. Joy did her best to keep a friendly smile on her face. She told herself everything would be fine. Joy knew that she could rely on Sara Beth to bring some good cheer to her day. She'd always been able to chase the darkest clouds away with one of her stories about growing up in Mudtown, Mississippi.

But as Joy perfected the display case for the day, she noticed that Sara Beth was strangely quiet. There were four regulars eating their morning pastries in the shop, and Sara Beth was usually a chatterbox with that sort of crowd.

"How are you doing today, Sara Beth?" a man named Joel asked between bites of his usual – the largest Danish Joy had available. The flavor didn't matter.

"I'm fine, Joel," Sara Beth responded. "Thanks for asking."

"Not very talkative today, are you?" a woman named Patsy pointed out.

"I guess I'm just tired." Sara Beth stepped away from behind the counter and wiped an empty table.

"You must be low on sweet tea today," Patsy insisted. "Why don't you pour yourself a glass, and sit down for chat like you usually do?"

"I'll need another Danish to keep me going if you're not going to give me any sugar, Sara Beth." Joel chuckled to himself.

"Yes, sir," Sara Beth answered cheerfully but robotically and made her way behind the counter again.

"I see that I'm not the only one freaked out about what happened yesterday," Joy whispered to Sara Beth.

"I dreamt about chocolate tarts last night." Sara Beth shrugged. "Normally, I'd welcome that sort of thing, but it was horrible."

Joy frowned and continued, "Well, I had nightmares too. I even got up thinking I heard someone breaking into the bungalow. Maybe it was the wind or something." Joy lied to herself to spare Sara Beth the stress.

"Well," Sara Beth said quietly. "That mocha cheesecake might help."

"It couldn't hurt," Joy agreed.

Joy let the issue go for now and took Sara Beth's advice. She sat at the bay window and ate a slice of mocha cheesecake to try and perk herself up. While she ate, she felt wide awake thanks to the bitterness of the coffee blending with the sharp tart flavor of the silky cheesecake. The bell above the door sounded. It was another regular named Coco. Sara Beth had often commented that Coco's big hair was just as big as her mouth.

"Sara Beth, my darling." Coco approached the counter and put a hand on her heart. "I just can't believe the news. Joy must be *devastated*."

"Morning, Coco." Joy waved from the bay window.

"Joy, honey," Coco responded so that the entire shop could hear her. "I'm so sorry about what happened. I just can't believe it. I really can't."

All eyes were on Coco. Sara Beth looked faint.

Joy joined her and Sara Beth at the counter, hoping to turn the volume of the conversation down a notch.

"Unfortunate things happen sometimes," Joy said.

"You must be devastated." Coco put a hand on Joy's shoulder and squeezed tightly. "Don't worry; I'll stand by you one *hundred* percent, no matter what Maple says."

"What do you mean by that?" Sara Beth suddenly perked up. "What did Maple say?"

"Oh, honey." Coco's volume rose again. "She told me the news. She's been telling everyone in town the sad, sad news."

"What news?" Sara Beth squeaked.

"What exactly has Maple been saying?" Joy pushed, her face flushed with curiosity.

"The terrible news about the ...," Coco lowered her voice, but everyone in the shop could still hear her, "... well, let's just say I'm surprised you're still selling those." She motioned dramatically to the chocolate tarts in the display case.

Sara Beth huffed.

"News of your chocolate tart scandal is all over town," Coco hissed. "Maple has been making sure of that. I don't normally listen to what she has to say, but I wanted to let you know I support you *one hundred percent.*"

"Well, I'd recommend you not listen to much of what Maple has to say since she has been out to get me since day one," Joy warned.

"I think it might be a bit late for that, Joy. I just can't believe you're closing the bake shop. I'm glad you're mother isn't here to see this." Coco flicked her poofy hair.

"What?" Joy exclaimed. "Maple has been saying that I'm closing the shop? Well, that's a lie."

"No one wants a poisoned pastry," Coco replied. Everyone in the shop slowly put down their forks and looked at their plates. Joel dabbed his mouth with a napkin and made a hasty exit. The rest of Joy's customers quickly followed.

"Hey, wait!" Joy called after them.

"Sorry, sister. I can't risk it with my bad liver." Patsy left cash on the table beside her half-eaten slice of vanilla pound cake.

Sara Beth gasped at the sight of the empty shop. Joy put her head in her hands and groaned.

"Well." Coco sighed. "What a shame. I'm with you *one hundred percent*, though. In solidarity, I'll take one of those rose water macarons, thanks. It's for the best, Joy, don't worry so much."

"How is it for the best, Coco?" Sara Beth asked snappily as she boxed up her sweets.

"The fewer customers you have, the less painful it'll be when you're shut down."

"Excuse me?" Joy looked between her fingers at Coco.

"But Maple said-"

"Well, you can tell Maple to ..." Joy took a deep breath to calm herself down. "Like I said Coco, we're not closing down. Not today anyway. And you can spread that rumor through town."

"Maple can come and see for herself that we're still here and as happy as ever to serve our perfectly safe, delicious, and renowned baked goods." Sara Beth put on a bright smile and led Coco towards the door.

"Oh, I'm not one for *gossip*." Coco clutched her box of sugary treats.

"Of course," Sara Beth replied with a polite smile on her face. "Enjoy the macarons. Thanks for coming in, Coco." Sara Beth wasted no time hurrying Coco out of the shop.

Joy and Sara Beth sat by the counter for an hour with their hands in their heads and watched through the big front windows as people crossed the street to avoid walking by the shop. Sara Beth gulped down an endless glass of sweet tea.

"There goes Mrs. Hunter." Joy sighed as she saw one of her favorite regulars approach the shop, change her mind, and scamper away towards the direction of The Sugar Room.

"Alright," Sara Beth slapped her hand on the counter, "We need a plan."

"Step one," Joy responded. "We wait for Detective Sugar to get back to us. Step two. We pray that the shop doesn't get into any more trouble."

"That's a horrible plan." Sara Beth slapped her hand on the counter again, forcing Joy to pay attention. "We need a plan of action." Sara Beth slapped the counter a third time again. "Ouch, that hurt. But do you get my point?" She cradled her hand.

"Go on."

"We have to find out what really happened," Sara Beth suggested.

"How are we going to do that?" Joy asked. "We're not police officers."

"That makes no difference. We can still conduct our own investigation." Sara Beth leaned in close to Joy and took an intimate sip of sweet tea. She continued in a hushed tone. "How did this Tony Florentine get his hands on one of our chocolate tarts? How was the tart poisoned? We need to at least try and figure it out."

"And if it brings the shop more problems?" Joy hesitated, but she knew that she couldn't let Patty Cakes Bake Shop crumble so easily. Her mother had put all of her time and hard-earned savings into making it what it was today.

"You're a brilliant baker, Joy." Sara Beth did her best to butter up her boss. "You make the flakiest pastries I've ever eaten, and I've been eating them for years and years. There is something *fishy* going on, and you know it."

Joy did know it. She knew it in her gut and her heart. Tony Florentine wasn't her fault, and the bake shop shouldn't be punished for the actions of the killer. Joy knew that staying in business wouldn't always be easy. She knew that one day she would have to fight for it just like her mother had.

"You're right, Sara Beth," Joy admitted. "There is something very, very wrong going on here. That detective did not give me a sense of confidence that he would get to the bottom of this himself."

"If he was a detective at all."

"I hadn't thought of that," Joy gasped. "Oh, wait. I did see his badge."

"Oh, right." Sara Beth shrugged. "I guess the way he snooped around the kitchen gave me the creeps."

"That's his job, I suppose," Joy replied.

"But he took your mother's spice blend." Sara Beth nodded and pursed her lips.

"Do you think –," Joy hissed. "Do you think all of this might be some colossal set up by The Sugar Room?"

"I don't know." Sara Beth sighed and took a huge gulp of sweet tea. "But we need to find out."

"We need to follow that chocolate tart." Joy grabbed her keys and began locking up. "Get Crystal's work address. It's about time we get started. We might as well do something with our morning."

"Yes, boss." Sara Beth saluted, and Joy noticed the excitement on her face.

CHAPTER FOUR

Sweetown Yoga Studio was housed in an space above a seaside cafe. Wafts of coffee grounds and caramelized sugar blew up the stairs into the studio, mixing with air from the sea.

Joy and Sara Beth shuffled awkwardly at the check-in desk as numerous women in yoga pants moved in and out of the hallways. They spotted Crystal seeing off her clients and making her way out of a big studio room. She had her hands in prayer position at her chest, and her high bun bobbled up and down as she bowed her head over and over again to each client, saying *namaste* to each one. Crystal spotted Joy and Sara Beth and bounced over.

"Ladies, I'm glad you're here." Crystal inhaled deeply as she reached her hands overhead, brought them back to prayer position at her chest, and suddenly dove into a deep forward fold.

"Namaste," she exhaled, barely making a sound with her lips pressed against her kneecaps.

"So flexible," Sara Beth whispered. "You must be so proud."

Joy nudged her.

Crystal stood quickly, jewelry jangling. She smiled and put a hand on Joy's shoulder.

"So glad to see you here, Joy. Yoga is a perfect hobby for someone like you who is so stressed all of the time."

"Yoga?" Joy coughed gently. "Actually we're here to talk about the chocolate tart we gave you."

"Oh, of course. Well, then I guess you've heard. Thank the stars Tony got to that tart first before I did." Crystal let out a soft laugh.

Joy and Sara Beth exchanged curious glances.

"You know Tony Florentine?" Joy asked.

"Yes." Crystal brought two fingers to the third-eye point of her brow. "Tony and I had a deep psychic connection at one point in time. We were-"

"Oh my gosh, you were lovers?" Sara Beth gasped, putting a hand on her heart.

"You must be devastated," Joy responded. "There's no worse time for things like this to happen than right before your wedding day."

"I'm fine. We hadn't seen each other for years. I was shocked when I sensed Tony's death, but his spirit helped me come to terms with it."

"Crystal," Sara Beth whispered, "you sensed his death?"

"Yes, I did." Crystal held her head proudly. "Also that handsome Detective Sugar came to question me this morning and told me all about

Tony's death. It's horrible, but it's also the circle of life."

"Oh." Sara Beth frowned. "So Detective Sugar told you all about the death." She, more than Joy, wanted to believe that Crystal had psychic abilities.

"Have you heard any rumors going through town about the incident?" Joy changed the subject.

"Oh Joy, you must be so stressed out," Crystal replied. "I heard your shop might be closing." Crystal began breathing rapidly, and her hands began to shake. "You are still able to do my wedding, right? Please, say you can. Please, don't close your bakery before my wedding. You have no idea how long it'll take me to find someone else. The Sugar Room has such a long waiting list, not that I *want* to do business with them. I just thought I should check since I heard you're closing and –," Crystal was on the brink of a full-fledged panic attack.

"We're not closing," Joy assured her, cutting her off.

"Do you promise?" Crystal took some deep breaths, exhaling through pursed lips. "Okay. Alright. I'm fine. Just fine." Crystal nodded between breaths to show that she was in control.

"I promise we're not closing," Joy explained. "That's just a rumor started by a desperate woman at The Sugar Room. We came here to ask you for any information you might have that could help us figure out who killed Tony Florentine. I mean, your ex-boyfriend."

Crystal nodded again and took hold of the front desk to steady herself through her deep breathing. Joy and Sara Beth looked at each other, cautious about whether they should keep asking questions. Crystal noticed and motioned with her hands to continue. Sara Beth took a notepad from her purse where they'd brainstormed questions on the drive over.

"I take it the detective asked you all kinds of questions about your relationship with Tony?" Joy asked.

Crystal paused, and then nodded. Sara Beth jotted down the response on her notepad.

"He seemed a little strange too if you ask me," Crystal informed them.

"What do you mean by that?" Joy waited for her to answer.

"He didn't try and flirt with me," she said quietly. "Not even once."

"Very strange," Sara Beth agreed, holding back an eye roll.

Joy continued with the questioning, "You said you hadn't seen Tony for years, and the detective said he died in his home. Do you have any idea how Tony could have gotten the chocolate tart?"

Crystal shook her head and exhaled a long sigh.

"Do you have any idea how the chocolate tart was poisoned?" Joy went on.

Crystal shook her head again.

"Do you know anyone who would have wanted to harm Tony?" Joy waited patiently, hoping that Crystal would have a solid answer to at least one of her questions.

"Crystal, who's this?" A woman approached the group and put an arm around Crystal's shoulders. Crystal immediately perked up, smiled and introduced her roommate, Kendra.

"Oh, you're the bakers," Kendra said. "So sorry to hear about the scandal. What a horrible thing to happen in our sleepy little town, even if Tony was a major creep."

Joy and Sara Beth pushed Kendra for more information.

"Tony was stalking Crystal," Kendra said bluntly. "But I doubt she mentioned that. She failed to mention that to the police too."

"Kendra," Crystal groaned.

"You said you hadn't seen Tony for years?" Joy repeated to Crystal.

"Oh, *she* never saw him," Kendra interrupted. "But I figured out it was him making all the weird phone calls and leaving weird gifts on our doorstep ever since Crystal got engaged."

"So, he left a gift or two," Crystal admitted. "It's a phase all of my ex-boyfriends eventually goes through."

"Look," Kendra said bluntly to Joy and Sara Beth. "Tony was a jerk with a temper. He got worked up when Crystal first started dating Lucas. I'm sure the news of their engagement crushed him."

"He probably was." Crystal sighed.

"Tony must have broken into the apartment, and for some reason took the chocolate tart in the process," Kendra suggested.

"I did leave a cute little note to Lucas on the box," Crystal confessed. "Maybe he saw it, and got angry."

"Were either of you home last night?" Joy asked.

"I dropped the chocolate tart off at home before coming to work. Kendra and I were both here teaching evening classes, and the chocolate tart was missing by the time we got back home." Crystal cleared her throat. "I was so annoyed that my darling Lucas wouldn't get to try any of that incredible chocolate, but now I know it was the will of the universe."

"That chocolate tart looked incredible," Kendra agreed. "And it was dairy-free too. It's such a shame."

A gong sounded suddenly.

"Oh, we need to get ready for our next classes." Crystal began untying and retying her hair into a higher bun. "Joy and Sara Beth, please stay for a class."

"Oh no –," Joy began.

"It's not really our thing," Sara Beth cut in, shaking her head.

"Please, it would mean so much to me," Crystal implored. "Today has been so hard. It will be such a comfort to have familiar faces in my class."

"You *must* try Crystal's class." Kendra echoed. "It's life-changing, I swear."

Joy and Sara Beth gave a few more excuses before finally giving in.

"I'll need a sweet tea after this," Sara Beth whispered.

"I'll need an entire cake," Joy replied.

CHAPTER FIVE

The yoga class began with everyone humming together. Crystal was at the front of the class on a slightly raised stage, sitting in a full lotus pose with her legs woven together. She led the humming by groaning into her headset. Joy and Sara Beth tiptoed their way through the lines of aspiring yogis sitting cross-legged and humming. The bakers were wearing sweats, and Sara Beth had ill-advisedly brought her handbag with her which jingled and clanked with every step. Joy shot her a look.

"Sorry," Sara Beth whispered. "I brought sweet tea just in case."

"Just in case of what?" Joy asked as they found two spare mats and settled themselves down.

"In case this class stresses me out even more," Sara Beth replied as she easily, and smugly, crossed her legs in front of her. Joy struggled to get her legs into a pretzel shape, and instead sat slouching until the humming was over.

"And breathe," Crystal instructed the class.

The beginning of the class was easy enough for Joy and Sara Beth. It consisted of rotating their heads from side to side and stretching their backs. Sara Beth felt herself relaxing into the stretches, and started to smile.

"And now let's relax into a downward dog position," Crystal instructed.

Joy and Sara Beth looked up to see what everyone else was doing and then looked at each other concerned.

"Form a sharp triangle shape with your body," Crystal breathed into the mic.

Joy and Sara Beth got the triangular shape for a moment, arms long and buttocks high, but quickly began to break a sweat. Their arms started to shake.

"Another thirty seconds," Crystal crooned. "Just *breathe*."

"Oh my gosh," Sara Beth whispered.

"This isn't so bad," Joy whispered back. "We can do this."

But the class escalated from a downward dog position, and into a standing sequence that highlighted how inflexible Joy and Sara Beth were. While the yogis around them were effortlessly lunging deeply into their warrior two poses, the women were practically upright with the stretch across their hamstrings burning.

"Now rest back into downward dog position and *breathe*," Crystal calmly announced. It was the most ridiculous thing Joy had ever heard in her life. There was no resting in this pose, but Crystal kept saying it in between the other poses that were admittedly even harder. All of them were back-breakers and leg-burners.

Joy's limbs were shaking, and Sara Beth was sweating so much that her mat became slippery. They were a hazard to their classmates. In dancer's pose, Sara Beth accidentally kicked the man behind her in the face. In tree pose, Joy toppled over into the woman next to her.

"I'm so –," Joy huffed, "I'm a hot mess of cake."

"If you get tired, or find these poses challenging…" Crystal began to tell the class in a soothing voice.

"Is she looking at us?" Sara Beth hissed to Joy.

"Who else would she be talking to?" Joy replied.

"Just move down into child's pose. And *breathe*." Crystal spoke deeply into the mic.

Joy and Sara Beth quickly followed her instructions, curling into balls on the floor and struggling to catch their breaths.

"All this oxygen is making me have crazy thoughts," Sara Beth wheezed.

"It's good for us," Joy agreed.

"What if," Sara Beth muttered quietly, turning her head to face Joy. "What if Crystal's fiancé Lucas is the killer?"

"Lucas?"

"Shhh, not so loud." Sara Beth glanced around. "Someone else here might know him."

Joy looked up and saw that the rest of the class was standing upright, and everyone seemed completely occupied with tying themselves into human knots.

"I suppose he would have a good motive if Tony were stalking Crystal," Joy admitted.

"Or if *stalking* means, you know," Sara Beth wiggled her eyebrows.

"I don't know." Joy frowned.

"Crystal says she and Lucas are *on and off* all the time. What if Crystal lied and she has seen Tony recently?"

"Oh," Joy replied. "Let's hope not."

"So what if Crystal was *on* with Tony, and Lucas found out about it?" Sara Beth raised her eyebrows.

"Or what if Tony was stalking Crystal, and Lucas wanted to protect her?" Joy added.

Crystal spoke loudly into the mic, "Everyone move down onto your mats for our final sequence."

"Finally, thank you," Joy said a little too loudly and rolled over onto her back. She stretched out, feeling every muscle in her body crying out for a warm bath or a dip in the ocean.

"Joy, we can't stay." Sara Beth was already packing up her things.

"Shoot. I completely forgot." Joy sat up in a hurry, remembering an important meeting she had with a brand new client.

A bottle of sweet tea dropped out of Sara Beth's bag and hit the floor with a *CLANG*.

"*Shhh,*" a neighboring yogi hissed.

Joy peeled her tired body off of the sweaty mat. She tiptoed out of the studio with Sara Beth, giving Crystal an apologetic smile.

But Crystal was busy breathing.

CHAPTER SIX

Joy had hoped that Crystal's yoga class would have helped her to sleep soundly that night, but it wasn't in the cards. She'd woken up several times during the night with strange sounds echoing through her head. Joy got up twice to investigate and, having found nothing, returned to bed only to be awakened shortly again soon after.

The next morning Joy woke up groggy and sore. Cheesecake trotted into her room and sat in a ray of sunlight, looking at Joy and purring. He looked sleepy too.

"I feel hungover, Cheesecake," Joy groaned.

Cheesecake purred in response.

"I have a huge wedding cake order to fill today." she sat up and grunted in pain as she felt how stiff her limbs were. "Mixing batters today will be a chore."

Cheesecake meowed, plopping down and curling up into the shape of a long bun.

"Sorry, I haven't brought you any fish lately, Cheesecake. It's been such a hard week." Joy gave the white cat scratches under his chin, and he began to purr. "Look at you. Not a care in the world. I bet you slept like a baby all night."

Cheesecake blinked at her sleepily.

Joy dragged herself out of bed and got ready for the day. She could barely get dressed. Her muscles were so tired and sore that she had to choose a dress that buttoned at the front and had no zip at the back. She made a silent promise to herself to stretch more and work on her flexibility once all of this wedding and murder investigation stuff was over and out of her life.

Making her way into town, Joy stopped off at the local market to stock up on snacks for the big baking day. She was loading a slab of sweet tea into her cart for Sara Beth when she suddenly saw a flash of tangerine orange in her peripheral vision. *Oh no,* she thought. The only person she knew who dared to wear such a flashy color was her nemesis, Maple McWayne.

Sure enough, Maple was making her way down the drinks aisle, inspecting each carbonated fruit juice she passed. Joy quickly dropped the sweet tea into her cart and sped around the corner. Joy moved quickly towards the registers, and repeated silently to herself, *please don't see me.* Up ahead at the end of the aisle, Maple stepped out in front of her.

"Joy!" Maple squealed. A fake smile graced her face. "What a joy it is to see you."

Joy's heart stopped, and she forced a broad smile.

"What a beautiful dress, Maple," Joy said, pushing her cart forward. She had to say something to keep herself from making a scene.

Maple did not step aside. Instead, she took hold of the end of Joy's cart and stopped it in its tracks. She leaned over it and locked her eyes onto Joy's.

"What terrible news," Maple breathed. "It was such a pity to hear about your little bake shop."

"Now Maple, we both know how that rumor got started." Joy spotted a regular customer coming down the aisle. "Patty Cakes Bake Shop is still very much open, and business is going well. Better than ever actually."

"Surely the murder investigation isn't good for business," Maple responded.

"Patty Cakes Bake Shop isn't to blame for what happened," Joy announced loudly down the aisle. "You can ask the detective on the case yourself. Like I said, business is booming."

"But *your* chocolate tart killed a man," Maple stated. "Your business is booming? I don't think so, dear." Maple fluctuated her tone wildly from whispering to near-shouting. "We've served many of your regular customers over at The Sugar Room since the scandal started. I can't imagine you're doing all that well. But perhaps you're right. Perhaps it has nothing to do with the poisoned chocolate tart *you* baked."

"It's funny to me how you take such an interest in my bakery," Joy commented snidely. "It's almost as if you're jealous or something."

"Why would I be jealous?" Maple barked back. "After all, my frosting was voted the #1 best frosting in town."

"You know very well that contest of yours was a scam." Joy narrowed her eyes. "Giving free cupcakes out at the senior center, and then asking them what they think doesn't count? Besides, you were the only bakery present. Please, what a joke."

"Oh, my goodness," Maple replied. "Are you alright, Joy? Your cheeks look like two slices of red velvet cake. Relax, dear. There's no need to get worked up over silly things."

If Joy's cheeks weren't red before then, they were now. Joy felt as if her blood was about to boil. She saw more customers lingering around the aisle, but she could barely keep herself together. Joy couldn't stand being in the same room as Maple.

"I'm fine." Joy casually laughed. "No need to worry, Maple."

"You should think about taking some time off," Maple suggested. "You know, take some time to relax. I mean I couldn't possibly with how many orders I've got to fill, but I'm sure it would do wonders for you skin."

"I'd be more relaxed if you stopped telling people that my bake shop is closing down when it most definitely is *not*," Joy responded. "Who would've thought that someone as *busy* as you would even have the time to run her mouth through town?"

The aisle was quiet.

"Excuse me?" Maple gasped.

"Oh don't act coy, Maple. I saw your car parked outside my shop that night, and you almost ran me over. I know you were involved somehow. You've been out to get me since day one." Joy clenched her fists. It was unlikely that Maple McWayne would ever dare throw a punch at her in public, but Joy was ready if she did.

"My car has been in the garage for over a week," Maple answered. "You must have mistaken me for someone else."

Thank you for your support! If you would like to know more about new releases and other fun things, sign up for my author newsletter by visiting my Amazon Author page.

Printed in Poland
by Amazon Fulfillment
Poland Sp. z o.o., Wrocław